Carol Arens delights in tossing fictional characters into hot water, watching them steam, and then giving them a happily-ever-after. When she's not writing she enjoys spending time with her family, beach-camping or lounging about in a mountain cabin. At home, she enjoys playing with her grandchildren and gardening. During rare spare moments you will find her snuggled up with a good book. Carol enjoys hearing from readers at carolarens@yahoo.com or on Facebook.

Also by Carol Arens

The Making of Baron Haversmere
The Viscount's Yuletide Bride
To Wed a Wallflower
'A Kiss Under the Mistletoe'
in *A Victorian Family Christmas*
The Viscount's Christmas Proposal
Meeting Her Promised Viscount

The Rivenhall Weddings miniseries

Inherited as the Gentleman's Bride
In Search of a Viscountess
A Family for the Reclusive Baron

Discover more at millsandboon.co.uk.

THE GENTLEMAN'S CINDERELLA BRIDE

Carol Arens

MILLS & BOON

First published in Great Britain 2023
by Mills & Boon, an imprint of HarperCollins*Publishers* Ltd,
1 London Bridge Street, London, SE1 9GF

www.harpercollins.co.uk

HarperCollins*Publishers*, Macken House, 39/40 Mayor Street Upper, Dublin 1, D01 C9W8, Ireland

The Gentleman's Cinderella Bride © 2023 Carol Arens

ISBN: 978-0-263-30527-2

07/23

MIX
Paper | Supporting
responsible forestry
FSC™ C007454

This book is produced from independently certified FSC™ paper to ensure responsible forest management.
For more information visit: www.harpercollins.co.uk/green.

Printed and Bound in the UK using 100% Renewable Electricity at CPI Group (UK) Ltd, Croydon, CR0 4YY

Dedicated to my sisters by marriage.

Karen, Joann, Elaine, Barbara and Jackie…
you are remarkable ladies, one and all.

Prologue

Mayfair, January 1875

For every widow a day came when she must put mourning behind her.

This was Clara Albright's day.

She pressed her back into the cushions of a big chair, took a fortifying breath, then gathered her resolve.

Her formal year of mourning had come and gone. Another year after as well. Now, at last, she was ready to let it go—in her sombre dress as well as in her heart.

Today she would put the last whispers of grief behind her...reawaken her happy spirit.

She had so much to be grateful for and she intended to rejoice over it. This was what her late husband would want for her. What he would expect of her.

'What do you think of this gown, Clara?'

Lilly, her seventeen-year-old sister, hurried across the parlour, then dropped onto the chair beside her in a great flounce of silk and lace. She pointed to a drawing in the *Ladies' Day Bazaar*.

'For my first ball after I have been presented.'

'It is exquisite. There is not a gentleman whose breath you will not steal. We shall summon the dressmaker in the morning.'

There was nothing like seeing Lilly's high spirits to ignite her own.

'We must order a gown for you too, Clara. You are too young to be a widow for ever.'

'I have decided to come out of mourning, but I have no intention of marrying again.'

She'd had her one true love. She could not imagine anyone living up to Spencer.

'You will need a man,' her sister said, still giving the greater part of her attention to the gown in the magazine. 'To keep you secure.'

'Thanks to my dear Spencer, I am quite secure.'

Her husband had left her with a great deal of money, which she had entrusted to the care of an accountant. And thank her dear Spencer for it. She knew nothing about finances.

And Spencer had left her with an even greater blessing than money.

Over by the fireplace her three-year-old daughter

was asleep on a cushion. A lock of red hair curled across her mouth, fluttering with her even breathing.

And there was George, her eight-year-old stepson, who was sitting in the bay of the window, frowning at the book open on his lap. His attention was more on the wind whistling though the bare branches beyond the glass than the words on the page.

What a sweet sight he was. Looking at him was nearly like looking at Spencer. George had been only a year old when Clara had stepped into the role of his mother.

Because her late husband had left her with so many blessings, both financial and people to love, her life was good. She was ready to get on with it.

Lilly would have her Season in society, the same as she would have had Spencer not passed away.

'Do you regret eloping and missing the grand, romantic adventure of a society wedding?' Lilly asked. 'Was it easy for you to give up what you might have had?'

'And what did I give up that was so grand? We were not the highest in society, Lilly. While our father was a baron, he was a poor one, and not of great influence. I did not give up anything that was wasn't worth it.'

'But eloping...?' Lilly hugged the magazine to her heart as if it were a talisman keeping her from committing such a blunder. 'Aunt Clarice and Uncle

Thomas shunned us because of it, and they were our only relatives.'

'I do not regret any of it. Not for one single second. And as far as our aunt and uncle are concerned, I am glad they are out of our lives. You recall how they constantly belittled us, even before I eloped?'

And now it was time to let her husband go. She had a family who needed all of her, not only what was left over from the grief.

'Well, I will never do that. Can't you see me as a duchess? Or perhaps a viscountess?'

'Easily.' Clara stood up, reached a hand down to her sister. 'But if you intend to catch yourself a duke or a viscount we should practise dancing.'

Lilly was already a lovely dancer—it was Clara who felt like taking a turn around the parlour, letting her soul fly joyful and free for the first time in two years.

'Which of us shall sing the tune?' Lilly asked.

'You sing. I will hum.'

So off they went, twirling about the room. Lilly was not singing, and Clara was not humming. How could they when they were laughing like a pair of cuckoos?

Life was suddenly bright again, filled with hope for sunshiny days to come. Days bright with butterflies flitting in flowers and bees humming in shrubs.

'Mama!' George called. 'There are constables coming up the steps.'

She and Lilly stopped, stared at one another.

Clara went cold to the bone.

The last time constables had knocked on her door it had been with the disastrous news of her husband's death.

The doorknocker clanked…clanked…clanked.

Chapter One

London, March 1877

Once upon a time Clara Albright had sparkled.

That had been one marriage and a loss of a fortune ago.

Now, walking past a smattering of clothes shops towards the food vendors' stalls, she smelled fish. This late in the day the aroma was ripe, but Clara was not deterred by it. This, she had learned, was the best time to haggle for a bargain.

Making her way down the pavement, she had to step around ragged-looking children playing hoop-and-stick. It broke her heart to see their dirty hair and their sallow skin. Many of them coughed from breathing the foul, ugly air.

It galled her that her own family was breathing the very same air. But curse her if the day should come when she would allow them to be dirty. Nor would the inside of the decrepit rooms they lived in ever look like the hovel it was.

Most of all curse her miserable, decency-forsaking, black-hearted accountant for stealing everything she had. That charming-as-a-saint villain had taken her money and robbed her of her sense of security. And she, as vulnerable as a new born mouse, had been unaware of him doing it. He'd accomplished it over a period of time and she, absorbed in her grief had not noticed.

Once again, an untimely knock on her door had brought ruinous news.

So no more sparkle for Clara Albright. Sadder but wiser, as the saying went.

Hopefully wise enough to get a fish and four potatoes for a price she could afford. The children were counting upon having dinner on their table tonight.

She approached the vendor, feeling the agitated knot which she got every time she walked this way grinding in her stomach. The fish seller's stall was in the very shadow of the factory Spencer had used to own. The very one that been sold by her criminal accountant.

Even after four years she tried not to look at it too closely. Ghosts came in and out of that factory door. Not vaporous images of the dearly departed. That was not what she saw. Rather, the ghost was her, or the woman she'd used to be, dressed in her fine gown and smiling her bright, innocent smile.

'Stuff and blather,' she mumbled, banishing the guileless woman she'd used to be.

Her family must eat.

'Good afternoon, Mr Horton.'

She shot the vendor a bright smile, in case it would influence his mood and make him look charitably upon her purchase. She'd catch more flies with honey instead of vinegar, and all that.

'I will take your largest fish and five of those sorry-looking potatoes behind you,' she said, even though their condition was not all that bad. This was but a step in the bartering.

The vendor made no move to gather her order, but narrowed a hard stare at her. 'That will be three pennies.'

'Are you in the habit of robbing your customers, sir?' More posturing. 'These fish have been sitting all day long. It will be a wonder if they are still fit to eat. I will give you a penny for the fish and the potatoes.'

'Please step aside, miss. I have other customers to help.'

Miss, was it? Two years ago it had been Mrs Albright, and he had fawned all over her, trying to attract her business each time she'd visited the factory.

Very well, she could not fault him overmuch for

not recognising her. Not when she, at times, did not recognise herself.

'I will give you a penny and a half,' she countered.

'For that I will give you a herring and one potato.'

Really, she should not let her temper prickle. Her situation was hardly his fault. If she cursed anyone it ought to be Miles Holmes. Who even knew where he was now? Cheating some other trusting widow, she supposed. If she ever encountered the scoundrel she would curse him with words she had yet to learn.

'Tell me, sir, how am I to feed a family of four with one skinny herring and a potato already growing eyes?'

The sun, slipping behind the factory roof, cast a long dark shadow over the pavement and the street. While the day was growing fearfully late, her timing for being here was just as she had planned it. The vendor would be anxious to pack up his goods and go home to his family.

'Sort through the herrings, if you will be so kind,' she said. 'I will need the largest of the barrel. Look through the potatoes as well. Find a nice plump one.'

Vendors to the left and right began to pack up, no doubt anxious to be off the streets before dark. While she had heard of vendors staying open late, she could not imagine it was safe.

Mr Horton cast a glance at the barrel of herrings,

frowned. 'A penny and a half for four potatoes and the herring?'

Not nearly enough food for the four of them. But she nodded, not wishing for him to hear disappointment in her voice. Hopefully she would finish sewing the gown she was working on and the customer would be quick paying for it. She prayed she would. Truly, her family needed more than one sad little herring for dinner.

She handed Mr Horton the penny and a half. While he wrapped the fish she looked up at the factory windows. How much had changed since Spencer had been in charge of it? Was there still the clinic she had set up for the employees? The food kitchen for those days when the time between paydays stretched long?

'Here you are, miss.' Mr Horton handed her the wrapped fish and the four potatoes. She put them in her bag.

'Good evening, Mr Horton.'

Walking away, she cast him a smile over her shoulder. Judging by the heavy weight of her bag, she was carrying home something rather larger than a herring. Tonight at dinner there would be a special blessing said for Mr Horton.

The wind began to blow. It whooshed down alleyways and howled around the corners of buildings, sounding a warning for her to hurry home.

Decent people were going inside for the night. In this part of town where she lived, only two streets away, thieves, scoundrels and women whose virtue could be bought for a coin would be emerging. In moments the streets would no longer be safe.

Footsteps tapped behind her, coming fast. Possibly it was a decent person, hurrying for the security of home. Just as possibly her basket was a tempting target for someone worse off than she was, and she was being pursued.

Her apartment came into view. She hurried towards the welcoming glow of the lamp in the window. The place was not much, but it was a haven from cold and crime. Being on the middle floor, it was more secure than having its front door exposed to the pavement. And when it rained water leaked though the roof into the attic rooms, not hers.

Longing for her old home, for her lovely, safe neighbourhood, was a waste of good time, and only served to make her curse fate again…or rather, her heartless accountant.

With the wind pushing at her back, she dashed up the steps and then hurried inside and up the interior staircase.

She rapped on the door once, and called, 'I'm home, my dears.'

If she knocked more than once, or spoke any other words, Lilly had been instructed not to open the door.

Fighting a great gust of wind, Andrew Benton closed the front door of his London townhouse, leaned against it and hung his head.

'Blight it!'

How the blazes was he to tell his mother that her darling youngest son was, at this moment, being carted off to prison?

He would not. Informing his mother that Miles was a thief of the lowest kind would crush her. And, having seen her crushed twice before, he wished never to see it again.

Andrew's father had died when he was ten years old, and his mother had become so depressed he had feared she would not come out if it. She had eventually, and then married a fellow she should not have.

His stepfather had turned out to be a charmer and a wastrel. 'Like father like son', the saying went. And as far as Andrew could tell, it was true.

When Parker Holmes had died, his mother had slipped into a decline from which the doctors had feared she would not rally. Andrew was not certain she had completely let go of her grief even after all this time.

Over the years he had protected her from what heartache he could, but this…

'It is just too blasted much!'

The butler emerged from the shadowed hall, giving him an odd glance. 'Sir?'

Andrew straightened away from the door, took off his coat and hat then handed them off.

'Forgive me, Jones. I should not have expressed my feelings so…' *Accurately* was what he wanted to say, but he let the word dangle.

As the son of a minister he had learned to display good character at a young age. He seldom cursed. No wonder Jones looked stunned.

'Is there any way I might be of assistance, Mr Benton?'

'Thank you, but no. Please do not worry about it. Do you know where my mother is? Has she retired for the evening?'

'No, sir, she is reading in the parlour.'

It was rather early for his mother to retire…the sun was only just setting.

'Will you send dinner to my brother's study and let my mother know I will not be joining her in the dining room tonight?'

'Certainly.'

One look at him and she would know something

was wrong. He needed time to gather himself, put on a happy mask for her sake.

Halfway across the hall Jones paused, turned around. 'Will your brother be returning tonight?'

'No, he will be gone for an extended period.'

'I understand.' Jones shook his head, frowned. 'I am sorry, Mr Benton.'

While no one spoke of Miles being on trial for embezzlement, it was hardly a secret. However, the small but loyal staff were quite discreet, understanding without being told that their mistress must not know of it.

'Shall I bring brandy with dinner?' the butler asked.

'Yes, Jones. I would appreciate that.'

Going to Miles's office at the back of the house, Andrew sat at his brother's desk, his forehead propped on fists clenched tight to keep them from trembling. Listening to wind blowing boisterously about the house, he let his mind go blessedly blank.

Blankness lasted for as long as it took him to remember the Dowager Wentworth's confused expression while attempting to testify at the trial. The elderly woman knew that her funds had been stolen, but every now and then she'd cast a smile at Miles, asking him if he knew who had done it. The evidence that it had been Miles had been clear, and he had been found guilty of the crime, but with the victim's confused testimony the sentence was a shockingly short eleven months.

How was he to explain those eleven months to his mother? Could he make up a story about Miles being on a long trip? Not the best of excuses, since Miles was not much of a traveller.

One thing was for certain: he would need to take Mother to their country estate, where keeping her out of gossip's way would be easier.

Jones delivered his dinner and brandy himself, rather than having Cook bring it. Thankfully his butler understood that he would rather see as few people as possible tonight.

A chore lay before him that he would rather run from than face.

It was unlikely that his brother had had a momentary lapse of character while keeping the Dowager's books. If he'd swindled one of his clients, he might have swindled more.

Miles had been a coddled rascal for as long as Andrew could remember. Somehow Mother had never seen beyond her second son's charm, just as she had never seen beyond his father's. When his mother loved, she did it quite blindly.

Andrew had seen the price she'd paid for that over the years. It was one of the reasons why, at thirty-five years old, he had only been in love one time. That one lesson had been enough to teach him to guard his heart.

Looking back, he was embarrassed at how besotted he had been by the perfectly lovely Edna Powers. He had declared his heart and eternal devotion to that woman. She had vowed the same to him. When one day she had not shown up for a romantic walk in the country, he had discovered it was because she had gone to London to wed a man with a title.

What a fool he'd been not to know she would do so. He was a commoner, she the daughter of a baron. Even if she'd meant the words of love she'd spoken, they were not worth anything.

Quite undone at the time, he had understood why his mother suffered as she did at losing love.

He'd understood. He had also learned.

As far as he was concerned, the time spent living in romantic bliss was not worth the painful months of getting over it. If the day came when he decided to marry, which he knew his mother counted on him doing, love would play no part in the arrangement. Walking in the clouds might be fine for some men, but Andrew preferred his feet on the ground.

Not that having his feet on the ground was all that pleasant at the moment. Because realistically he knew if his brother had cheated one widow, he had cheated another.

If so, it fell to Andrew to make amends.

Taking a slow sip of brandy, then a bite of bread, he set to the task of searching out the truth, as ugly as he expected to find it.

Opening drawers, shuffling through the contents of each one, he was relieved he had never given his brother responsibility for the family finances. One captain per ship was what Andrew believed, and he had been captaining this ship since before his brother had had fuzz on his chin.

At one point Miles had come home from college, full of self-importance, arguing that he was the one who should be in charge of the family's money. He'd puffed up his chest and pointed out that he was the one studying arithmetic at college. Andrew had pointed out that he was the one paying for it.

Thank the good Lord that he had not given over a single ledger to his brother's care. A man who was worm enough to cheat a widow might swindle his own family.

Andrew had worked long and hard to build his business of buying fine fabric from around the world and then selling it to factories in London. There was a great deal of profit in doing so. One thing he had learned from his late stepfather was that financial security was essential, seeing as he had nearly robbed them of it. Andrew had always been diligent in making sure Mother would be secure.

As he poked about here and there, Andrew did not like thinking his brother so heartless as to—

What was this? A locked drawer?

It might contain nothing more than private correspondence. After all, his brother was a lady-charmer. What was inside might only have to do with his liaisons.

Somehow, Andrew feared it did not.

He nearly knocked his dinner plate off the desk in his haste to find a key.

If there was one, it was well hidden.

A locked drawer and a hidden key...not an indication of honesty.

The creeping certainty that Miles was concealing other crimes made Andrew feel sick as sin.

Standing, he glanced about for something to prise open the drawer. Miles's office contained books, statues and artwork, but nothing that would serve as a crowbar. He could go outside to the small stable in the yard to find a tool, but it was blustery. Not only that, he was much too impatient to take the time.

He studied his shoe, shrugged, then lifted his leg and kicked at the drawer. It caved in, making it no great feat to pull off the front.

Rolling the drawer all the way out, Andrew lifted it,

then dumped the contents on top of the desk. A bundle of ledgers was bound by a rubber band. He lifted it up.

Andrew recognised the name of the client: Clara Albright. There had been a time when he'd conducted business with her husband, selling him quality fabrics. He had met the lady on a couple of occasions, and recalled her being a lively and gracious hostess.

There had been one occasion, when attending the opera with his mother, when he had run into the Albrights. His conversation had been mostly with Mr Albright, having to do with business. But his attention had been drawn to Mrs Albright, and how the woman had sparkled when she gazed at her husband.

At the time he'd thought her devotion to her husband to be enchanting…but worrisome too. Enchanting because what man would *not* want to be loved that way? Worrisome because Andrew knew what would come of giving so much of oneself to another person. He'd brought his mother through her losses, and had brought himself through one too.

It was a risky dream Mrs Albright lived, he had thought. Not that she was likely to be aware of the danger.

Later, when he'd heard of Mr Albright's passing, he'd been sorry to know he had been right. The lady had been happy for such a short time before she had paid the price of loving. And now he feared that Miles had stolen her money. A double blow for Mrs Albright.

How had she fared? Perhaps she'd had family to take her in, as was often the case. Not that it in any way excused what his brother had done. No matter how well her circumstances might have worked out, it was his duty to find her and make his brother's crime against her right. Even if the lady had remarried he owed her justice…in as much as he could offer it.

But until he spent more time delving into his brother's dishonest dealings he would not know the extent of it.

Hours later, Andrew bent his forehead to the desk. He was a man who did not curse, but the echo of profanity vibrated hotly against the polished wood.

The notation his brother had made at the bottom of this page, with his own hand, indicated that the widow, her daughter, her stepson and her sister had been turned onto the street.

Two years ago!

The cheerful flourish of Miles's penmanship gave no sense that he was remorseful for leaving the family destitute. It was sickening to imagine his brother might be proud of what he'd done. But it must be the truth. Why else would he have written about it? Bragged about it?

Even if he managed to find Mrs Albright, and repaid her three times over what Miles had taken from her, it would never be enough. Surely her sense of security must have been stolen along with her money. And feeling safe in the world was not something money could replace.

If a woman's money had been stolen once by an unscrupulous man, the fear of it happening again would surely weigh upon her. London had more than its share of scheming reprobates on the hunt for helpless widows to cheat.

He knew what poor women went through—had seen it as a child. Andrew had often accompanied his father on charitable missions. He'd even worked alongside him, trying to improve the lives of unfortunate children and women. Trying and often failing.

His mother had used to think his father should not expose him to the uglier side of life. But it existed, whether he was exposed to it or not.

The only thing Andrew regretted was being only half the man his father was.

It was charity that had killed him in the end. He had caught a disease at the poorhouse he'd served. And from that day on his mother had ended his visits to the poor. He'd obeyed her because of her grief and his fear of making it worse.

Sick at heart, he pounded his fist on the desk. What

had become of Mrs Albright? Had she ended up in the poorhouse? The children sent to an orphanage?

At least when Miles had robbed the Dowager, her wealthy son had been there to step up for her, to see Miles brought to justice. It appeared that Mrs Albright had no one to do that for her—otherwise she would not have been put out on the street.

Blighted blazes.

But there was nothing to be done about it tonight. If there had been he would do it.

His goose-down mattress was going to feel like horsehair with all the guilt he carried.

Even Miles might be sleeping in a more secure place than Clara Albright and her family.

Leaving his brother's study, he found Jones slumped in a chair in the corridor. Apparently the butler had fallen asleep, waiting to see if Andrew needed anything.

He touched Jones's shoulder. 'Off to your rest, man.'

'Is there nothing more you need, sir?'

'Not tonight. But in the morning, please cancel all my appointments.'

It was not clear in Andrew's mind what he was going to do with his time, but it would certainly have something to do with locating the cheated widow. Whatever it took to make this right with her, he would do it. And the 'whatever' playing in his mind did not have so much to do with restoring her funds but rather restoring her sense of security.

That, he knew, was the worst of what his brother had taken from her.

Trudging up the stairs to his chamber, he seemed to ache all over, from his heart to the tips of his toes. The only thing that gave him relief was knowing that he would ensure no lowdown charlatan would have the opportunity to take advantage of Mrs Albright again.

But it was a tricky business he was getting into.

He rather doubted she was going to trust the brother of the man who had ruined her.

It would probably take time and patience to convince her to accept what he had to offer. Luckily, he had an abundance of both.

Chapter Two

'Is there something you want, Lilly?' Clara asked, her needle poised over the stitch she was about to make.

Her sister stood behind the chair, watching over her shoulder and blocking the lamplight Clara needed to work by.

'That gown.'

She glanced up to see Lilly's arms folded across her chest and her green eyes filled with longing.

'I want that gown.'

'If I give it to you we will not eat next week.'

Lilly spun away, strode to the window and stared at the rain streaking down the panes.

'If I do not have a gown I will not be able to join society and find a husband.' Her sister cast a frown over her shoulder. 'We will be much better off if I find a wealthy gentleman.'

Clara set the gown aside, and joined her sister at the window.

'Having a wealthy husband will not ensure financial security. We know that, do we not? Look for a man who pleases you, Lilly. Happy memoires keep you warm at night. Money does not.'

'Money buys plush blankets, which also keep one warm at night. I, for one, would rather have memories of wealth than poverty. Anything will be better than living like this. Besides, simply because we were ruined once, it does not mean we will be again.'

Clara brushed a strand of her sister's golden blonde hair away from her cheek. Life had not treated Lilly the way she had expected it to. Clara understood her despair. Growing up, she had believed she would one day wed a peer, and now she was reduced to choosing between the butcher's son and the fisherman's lad.

Well, no wonder she was distressed...

Still, being wed to a peer or a common man, the risk of ruin was as great.

'Lilly, I am sorry. You know I cannot give you this gown. Besides, there is only one way for you to be financially secure. Learn a skill and attend to the lessons I have given you regarding money. Learn to be the mistress of your own funds. We have learned how it ends when a lady is ignorant of her finances.'

'I will sew gowns alongside you, Clara. I will also learn to manage what money we take in. But it is not what I wish to do until my dotage.'

'I shall go to work in Father's factory,' George declared, tugging on Lilly's skirt to get his aunt's attention. 'Then I shall buy you a gown.'

This was not the first time Clara's ten-year-old stepson had made such a declaration. It was sweet of him, but...

'You are the dearest boy I know,' Clara told him. 'But you will do no such thing. You will continue to attend the Ragged School and learn a better way to earn money.'

It was not as if she could afford to send him to an upper-class school such as the one he would have attended had her fortune not been stolen.

Clara had half a mind to teach him at home, where she could keep him safe. So many poor children attended the Ragged School. She could not be sure George would not catch a childhood ailment or worse.

It was not as if she could afford to pay a doctor if he became ill. And heaven forbid he should bring something home to his younger stepsister. Annabeth's health was delicate as it was.

However, she owed it to Spencer to make sure his son grew up to be a proper gentleman. One day a prosperous one.

Despite the fact that her days were consumed with stitching garments for the well-to-do, she always took the time to walk George to school and then bring him home again. Oh, he protested that he was old enough to go alone… However, these were rough streets. No matter how he argued that he was nearly a man, she meant to protect her late husband's child until he grew a moustache and a beard. A full, thick beard…

Heavy footsteps pounded up the interior staircase.

They all fell quiet, glancing at one another.

The staircase serviced one other dwelling besides theirs before it led to the attic rooms.

Having become acquainted with her neighbours, she knew that such heavy plods did not belong to any of them.

'Just because someone is coming up the stairs it does not mean it has to do with us,' Lilly said, wringing her hands. 'Are we terribly behind on the rent?'

'Not terribly…'

Or not so late that the landlord would come knocking. Even if he did, she and Lilly would have the gown finished in two days, and the rent would be the first thing paid.

'Someone walking past our door does not mean disaster.'

'Perhaps he is going to knock on Mr Mawbry's door and bring *him* disaster?' suggested five-year-old Annabeth.

Annabeth had been a baby the first time disaster had knocked, and three years old the second time.

Her daughter did not remember the life they'd had before this one. The only reason she feared strangers at the door was that she had picked up on it from the rest of them.

'Anybody coming out in this storm will be bringing bad news,' George declared, and took a place between the door and the women of his family.

'I am sure whoever it is will pass us by,' Clara assured them.

Knuckles hit the door. *Knock-knock. Knock-knock.*

Clara put her finger to her lips, indicating they should keep quiet. Perhaps the visitor would think them not at home.

The knock came again, heavier this time.

'Mrs Albright!' A deep voice called. 'I am Andrew Benton. May I have a word?'

Benton? The name sounded as if it ought to be familiar, but the reason for that escaped her. And until she remembered the door would remain locked. They would continue to pretend not to be at home.

Benton was not an uncommon name... Perhaps that was why it was familiar.

Andrew Benton knocked again. 'Mrs Albright?'

'The lamp is on,' George whispered. 'He knows we are here.'

'Just because a man comes to the door it does not mean he is bringing horrid news,' Lilly pointed out.

'I am sure that is true,' Clara whispered back.

Except that respectable callers came during daylight hours—especially in this neighbourhood. And anyone delivering good news, or even average news, would not come during a storm.

'I must speak with you. And it is challenging through the door.'

'If you wish to order a suit please come back during proper hours.'

Perhaps the reason for his visit was simply that. It was only his sense of proper timing which was at issue.

'A suit? No... I have news of Miles Holmes. I thought you might be interested to hear it.'

Crossing the room to the lamp, Clara turned the wick low.

Andrew had his mouth open to press again the reason for his visit, but then he saw the light leaking between the door and the frame go out.

He couldn't blame Clara Albright for not receiving him. She was correct about the hour being improper for callers. And if he could do it over again he would not have mentioned Miles right away.

No wonder she did not wish to speak with him if it had to do with the man who'd swindled her.

Stepping back down the dark, creaky staircase, he conceded defeat for the night. Not for ever, though.

Through the detective he had hired to gather information about Mrs Albright he had discovered where she lived, who lived with her, and what she did to support them all.

Miles had not left them in comfortable circumstances.

No gently bred woman should be called upon to live in this area of London.

No woman of any standing should, as far as he was concerned.

But he could not help them all. He could help this one, though…was duty-bound to do so.

It was no wonder she did not open her door. He might have been a hooligan or worse. And she with a sister and two young children to protect.

One thing he had learned about Clara Albright was that she was no longer the delicate society lady he had met. She had risen to the challenge set before her, and so far no one belonging to her had starved.

It was his intention to make sure no one did, and to ensure that she never needed to fear who came to her front door again.

Also to make sure that her front door was in a more appropriate area.

But clearly he was not going to put her heart at ease tonight with his news about Miles being in prison. Tomorrow afternoon he would come back and present his well thought-out and sensible proposition about making amends.

He might need to commission a new suit in order to gain an audience with her. But from what he'd learned about her she did excellent work. Not that it made her enough money to live comfortably. She lived from hand to mouth. And if there had been any doubt about his investigator's report, seeing where she lived had put it to rest.

At the bottom of the stairs, he opened a door which led outside to the steps down to the pavement.

It was not the pouring rain which made him hesitate to dash to his carriage, waiting for him at the kerb. It was the pair of unsavoury-looking fellows staring at his carriage from across the street which gave him a second's pause. They would not be aware that a burly coachman was inside, sheltering from the rain.

As soon as Hinton saw Andrew trotting down the steps he emerged from the cab. Andrew tipped is head in the direction of the men, in order to alert his driver to their presence. Hinton shot them a deep nod and a big, toothy grin. His massive presence was enough to send the men scurrying around the corner.

Within seconds Andrew was secure in his carriage and being carried to the safe streets of Mayfair. Not that it gave him much comfort. He was all too well aware that while he rode towards his safe, comfortable home, men like those ones had just encountered would be lurking on corners and in shadowed doorways just beyond Mrs Albright's front door.

And it was his brother's fault that she was there. Tomorrow he would set it all to rights.

In the meantime he would kneel beside his bed and pray that the woman and her family were not accosted during the night.

With the room safely dim, Clara stood beside the window and pulled aside the tattered shade.

The man who had been at her door went out of the building and got into a carriage. A fine carriage of the sort that she, at one time, had ridden in.

The conveyance had caught the attention of a pair of thugs lingering on the corner. She had half a mind to rap on the glass and alert her visitor to them, but in that instant a large man stepped out of the carriage. The villains slunk around the corner.

How interesting that the carriage driver had waited within the cab and not on the driver's bench, wrapped in an oilcloth against the rain.

It was wise to be suspicious of the stranger who had come to her door, but at the same time if he was a decent sort, caring for the wellbeing of his employee, that needed to be recognised as well. Perhaps the visitor was not a villain and he need not be feared.

Whatever the case, it did not matter. Since the man he'd mentioned, Miles Holmes, *was* a villain. If he meant to present the miscreant in any other light he was not welcome at her door.

Once the driver had closed the door and taken his place on top the fine carriage rolled away. No doubt to some safe, affluent home.

'We've seen the last of him.' Making the announcement, Clara reached for the lamp and turned up the wick.

'I wonder what he wanted,' Lilly said, peeking around Clara and then drawing aside the window shade to look.

'If it has to do with our former accountant, we do not want to know.'

'*I* might want to.' Lilly straightened. 'It is curious… him coming here.'

Annabeth coughed from her pallet beside the hearth. Clara added a few lumps of coal to the fire and the room warmed quickly.

'Time for bed, George. Morning will come soon enough, and you need your mind to be rested for school.'

Bed for George was a corner of the kitchen, where the heat radiating from the fireplace bricks helped to warm him.

'If I worked at the factory I would not need my mind rested.'

With a hand on his shoulder she guided him towards the kitchen. 'If you worked at the factory you would be up far earlier than you must be for school.'

She kissed his cheek and watched him shuffle into

the kitchen out of sight. She listened to the blankets on his cot rustle, the wooden legs creak and moan as he settled.

Lilly came and sat in the chair beside hers, reaching for the sewing basket.

'Get some rest, Lilly. I will not have you too weary to see to your bookkeeping lessons.'

'You will come soon?' Lilly rose, and walked towards the bedroom the women shared.

'Quite soon.'

After her sister had gone into the bedroom, Clara let out a sigh to express how weary she was. She pressed back in her chair, picked up her sewing.

'Close your eyes, Annabeth. I will carry you to bed when I go.'

Her daughter always slept between her and Lilly for extra warmth. March could be terribly cold and damp, and Annabeth was frail.

For all the misery Miles Holmes had caused her family, she resented what he had done to Annabeth most intensely. Her child had been vigorous before they'd been forced to move into these squalid rooms.

While stitching a flounce of lace on a pearl-dotted hem, she thought about people...how some were so much better off than she and some were so much worse off.

It had been an act of Providence, she had always

thought, finding this place on the very day they'd been evicted.

Her cook, a good and kindly lady, had known of the vacant rooms because her sister had moved out of them that same morning. Cook had spoken to the landlord and made arrangements for them to move in, and had even loaned her the money for their move.

Had it not been for Cook, she and her family would have spent that night huddled in an alley.

Even though the rooms were humble, they had a roof and walls. For that, she was grateful.

The very night they'd moved in, with the wind howling and the rain coming down, she had made a vow that she would never complain. Because complaining earned nothing but dissatisfaction. What she'd also vowed to do was work hard, from before dawn until after her family was asleep. That was the path to survival.

Looking back was futile, and only broke one's heart.

Looking ahead was a waste of time, since one's road could never be predicted.

The only way forward was to make one's way one step at a time. Or rather, one stitch at a time…

At ten o'clock the next morning Andrew stepped out of his coach. Hopefully Mrs Albright would consider this an appropriate hour to receive visitors. The urgency of what he had to say to her did not lie easily on his mind.

The wind tugged at his trousers, sent swirls of cold air up his legs. But thankfully the rain had stopped. Standing at the foot of the steps he wondered how sound the building was.

He gave the bottom step a swift, hard kick. Wincing, he decided he ought to have worn sturdier shoes. But it was good to know that the step would not collapse under anyone soon.

Which was not to say the roof would not cave in... Its shingles were curled, looking old and splintered, and if one looked closely enough—which he was doing—one would notice that the roofline sagged.

Climbing the creaking interior stairs to the middle floor, he was glad that Clara Albright and her family would not be residing here much longer. As soon as he'd had a word with the lady, and presented his proposal, he would arrange for the family to move.

He knocked on the door. 'Mrs Albright? It is Andrew Benton. I hope this is an appropriate hour for us to speak.'

A pair of women's voices issued from behind the door. Although they were muffled, he could tell that one of them was arguing in favour of speaking with him and the other against.

While they discussed it, the door opened a crack and a small girl peered up at him.

'Do you wish for Mama to sew you a suit, sir?'

'Annabeth!'

Suddenly the door opened wider. The child disappeared behind a worn and patched skirt. Andrew looked at a face whose features were familiar. But to say that this was the woman he remembered would be wrong.

The Clara Albright he recalled had had a smile which enveloped a person in welcome.

This Clara Albright had a frown which all but erected a spiked fence between them.

'If you have something to say about Miles Holmes you may speak to the other side of this door, sir.'

She started to slam it in his face, but another feminine hand held it open. This one must belong to the lady who wished to give him a chance to speak. The younger sister, he guessed. Lilly...that was what the investigator had said her name was.

'What is it, then?' Mrs Albright cast a frown at her sister and then one at him.

Where once there had been an engaging sparkle in Clara Albright's eyes there was now suspicion. Unless he missed his guess, she was gathering an arsenal of words with which to assault him.

Miles had done this to her. Changed the sparkle to jagged shards.

The urge to punch his half-brother in the chin was rather strong, his father's teaching on turning the other cheek notwithstanding. He might have managed a more charitable attitude had the injured cheek been his own…

'To begin, I would like to tell you that Miles is in prison, serving time for stealing the fortune of another widow.'

The lady did not seem as pleased to learn the news as he'd expected. With her fists curled tight at her waist, she lifted her chin and levelled a hard gaze upon him. Not an easy feat since he was a head taller than she was.

However, her attitude did manage to make him feel smaller, which was clearly what she intended. While he was obviously conversing with Clara Albright, she was not the same pampered lady he had met in the past. Not by any means. He began to fear she would not welcome what he had to say next.

'Please explain, Mr Benton. How do you know that I am a widow and that I have been robbed of my fortune?'

'Because it is my brother who has robbed you.'

She stepped into the corridor and closed the door behind her. The door across the corridor creaked open.

An elderly man poked his head out. Whether out of curiosity, or to be helpful to his neighbour, Andrew had no way of knowing.

'Mrs Albright, if this gentleman is pestering you, say the word and I shall escort him off the premises.'

'Why, thank you, Mr Mawbry.'

Mrs Albright cast her neighbour a smile. It looked as warm and lovely as he remembered from the past.

'You shall be the first person I will call if I require help.'

The old gentleman gave Andrew a severe nod, then closed his door again. As soon as it clicked shut the sparkle faded from the lady's eyes. Her frown was set upon him as sharply as if he had delivered bad news.

But just the opposite was true. He meant only good. To lift this worrisome existence from her shoulders and make her safe once again.

'Since you have delivered the message about your brother, I wish you a good day.'

Clearly she wished him nothing of the kind. But once he'd finished saying what he needed to, he hoped her attitude would change.

'May I have a moment more, Mrs Albright?'

'I am rather busy.' With a curt nod she reached for the doorknob. 'Again, thank you for letting me know about Mr Holmes.'

'I wish to make amends for what my brother has done to you,' he said quickly.

She let go of the doorknob. 'Amends? I'm sure that is an honourable thought, sir, but I hardly see how the past can be altered.'

'You are correct. The past cannot be changed. I mean to address the present…and the future.'

'And how, exactly, do you intend to do that? Purchase my old home and give it back to me? Restore my bank account and somehow wipe my memory clean of your brother's treachery?'

Here was his moment. At last he would see her smile the way she'd used to. Not that she likely remembered doing so at him, since she'd used to smile at everyone. But in seconds the burden of guilt he carried for her circumstances would be lifted.

'I wish to offer for your hand in marriage.'

She did smile—but in the oddest way. And then she laughed.

'It's a bold one you are.' She opened the door, shook her head. 'Heaven help me. One brother a scoundrel and the other mad. Good day to you, Mr Benton!'

With that, he found himself staring at the splintered paint on her door.

Chapter Three

Marry him? The brother of her nemesis? A man who, while as handsome as a long sunny day, was not in his right mind? What could he have meant by saying such a thing to her?

The mystery occupied her mind all day long.

The best she could think was that mental imbalance ran in the Benton family.

Walking towards the Ragged School to collect George, she decided to strike it from her mind. As best she could, at least. It was unsettling that he had gone to the trouble to hunt her down and offer such an outrageous proposition.

Marriage? The man was daft and beyond!

Truly, she could ask anyone and they would agree. Mr Benton was not right in his mind.

And at the moment she had no time to dwell on Mr Benton and his nonsense. She had a child to bring home from school and then a trip to the fish market.

All before dark. And after that, a gown to finish so that they would be able to eat next week.

She would think of Mr Benton no longer. Except... how could she not?

Seeing George come out of the building which had been donated for the Ragged School, she hurried towards him. 'How was your day, George?'

What was that? Blood welled on his bottom lip.

Turning his face this way and that, she asked. 'Were you in a scrape, young man?'

'It wasn't my fault.'

'And whose was it, then?'

'Hunter Monroe's. He's a bully. Not the only one, either. I should not be at school. I should be working at my father's factory.'

Although he was ten years old, she took a firm hold of his hand, leading him home. 'And do you think there are no bullies at the factory? There are—and they are bigger than the ones at school.'

'The money would be worth a small bruise or two,' he grumbled.

Have mercy...

She sent a thought to Spencer. *I am trying my best to bring him up properly, but if there is anything you can do from up there, I would not take it amiss.*

Climbing the stairs to their rooms, she gave her customary knock.

'It's only us,' George called.

The door flew open wide, revealing both Lilly and Annabeth, grinning widely.

'The most wonderful thing has happened!' said Lilly.

'I cannot imagine what… George, go and wash your face, then begin your studies. You can tell me after I return from the market. It will be dark when I return as it is.'

'You don't need to go to the market, Mama.' Annabeth clasped Clara's hand and drew her towards the tiny kitchen. 'Look! A box was left at the door.'

Indeed… A large box sat square on the kitchen table. What on earth…?

'There is food in it,' Lilly said, drawing out a loaf of bread and holding it up as if it was the grandest of prizes. Which it was. 'There's cheese and sausage, too.'

'And cake!' Annabeth jumped up and down so joyfully that it made her cough.

'Here, Clara, there is a letter for you,' said Lilly. 'It was in the box.'

'Did you see who brought the box?' she asked. This was too strange for her to simply cheer their good fortune.

'It was the grocer's lad. I saw him through the window, carrying it up.'

That could not be all there was to it.

'And did you see anyone else through the window?'

'Well, if you must know, I did. It was the man from yesterday... Mr Benton. He directed the boy to bring the box up.'

What a fine pickle this was. She did not want to have anything to do with the odd man, and yet she could hardly turn away perfectly good food.

Then again, if she did turn it away it would make a point to Mr Benton. She and her family were not for sale. If his intention was to lure her that way. Except she could not imagine why he would want to.

Still and all, she would not refuse food which would save her a trip to the market. Which would also keep the money she would have spent nicely in her purse.

'We haven't had cheese in an age,' Clara said, gazing in pure longing at the cheese wheel.

There had been a time in her life when cheese had been commonplace. Now it looked as if it were made of gold. Better than gold. One could not eat gold.

She ought to read the letter before dinner, just to be certain she was not obligating herself to something. Marriage, for instance.

'Please serve the children, Lilly. I will eat later.'

Turning up the lamp, she sat down on her chair, unfolded the letter.

My dear Mrs Albright,
Please accept my apology for bungling things as
I did yesterday.

She grunted aloud, which made her family look up briefly from their feast. Bungling, indeed. At least he recognised the fact. Andrew Benton might not be completely insane. Perhaps he was simply possessed of incredibly bad judgement.

I did not express, as I ought to have, the deep regret I bear for my younger brother's treatment of you. There is no excuse for him. If it were not for fear that my mother would discover it, I would be happy he is spending time in prison. While his sentence is not for the crime against you, it does serve...

She set the letter on her lap. He was a man who had concern for his mother. Hmm... She would bear that in mind.

She picked up the letter again.

...as a form of justice. But what I propose is to give you back what you have lost. I understand it might not be possible entirely. Time lost cannot be regained, I am aware.

'He does not seem as insane in his letter as he did in person,' she mumbled.

'He did not seem insane to me, Clara,' her sister called.

It was a small room, and nothing could be muttered in private.

'He must be. Otherwise… Well, never mind.'

'Maybe you should give marrying him some thought. He must live somewhere better than here. And his carriage looks rather fine. I do not doubt that he can afford a gown or two.'

Lilly must have had her ear pressed to the door to know about his proposal.

'Perhaps you should marry him,' said Clara.

'He did not ask me.'

She continued to read.

Before you rip up my letter and toss it in the fireplace, I ask, once again, for your hand in marriage. We are not strangers in the strictest sense. I did business with your husband upon occasion. You and I have met a couple of times.

Perhaps not strangers in the strictest sense, but in the real one—yes, indeed they were.

I realise how outlandish this must sound to you. It is only that I know of no other way to make up for my brother's crime.

He could simply pay her back what Miles had taken. Had that not occurred to the man?

Be assured that I can well afford to wed. I will
call again to discuss the matter further. I hope
you will not close the door on me this time, for
my offer is sincere. I am not insane.
With most sincere regards,
Andrew Benton

Perhaps insane had been a hasty pronouncement. But he certainly had an exaggerated sense of guilt if marriage was his way of easing it.

If he appeared at her door again she would not send him away immediately. He had gone to a great deal of trouble to present his offer. She would give him a few moments, during which she would make it clear that marriage was the last thing she would consider.

She'd had the love of a lifetime. Spencer had been enough of a man to last her the rest of her days.

There had been no hint of affection in the letter, naturally. Apparently he had met her once or twice, but she did not recall him at all. She was not sure she even liked Andrew Benton.

Rising, she went to the fireplace and tossed the letter into the coals with a flourish.

Then a thought crept into her mind—and not one she welcomed.

If Andrew Benton was financially comfortable, as his fine carriage would suggest, and if she accepted his proposal, she would not need to count every piece of coal she added to the hearth. Also, if anything were to happen to her, her family would be safe with him. As matters stood now, without her they would come to utter ruin.

But perhaps she was the one who was insane to even consider marriage to a perfect stranger.

If there was one thing she was not, it was insane.

The next day Clara returned home from collecting George from school to find a feast upon her kitchen table. Two cooked chickens, two mince pies, a bowl of steaming cabbage and a great smile upon Annabeth's face.

Indeed...a great smile and a smear of chocolate.

Apparently Mr Benton had brought a cake, and her daughter had taken a finger-swipe at it.

How interesting that he had not remained to be thanked for bringing the food. Although it might be coincidence. Nothing more than timing.

However, if he thought she would turn away perfectly fine food if she was at home when he delivered it...

Ha! It seemed to her that a man ought to know a woman better than that before he proposed marriage. She might be proud, but she was not a fool.

As far as marriage went, it was not something she

would consider without knowing him better. And even if she did know him better she would still refuse.

The fact that Andrew Benton was the brother of the man who had ruined her could hardly be dismissed.

Nor could the fact that she was not willing to give over her financial security to a husband.

As pitiful an amount of security as it was, it was hers to account for. Hers to guard and protect, much as a mother bird guarded the eggs in her nest.

She had learned the lesson of trusting another bird with her nest in the most painful way imaginable. With that learning had come independence, along with pride in her hard-won accomplishments.

And yet smelling the aroma of food on the dining table, knowing she could not have afforded it on her own, gave her pause.

In the end it was the chocolate on Annabeth's grinning face which made her give way to a smile. A smile which sprang from her heart in the most curious way.

It was nearly as if the girl she'd used to be was knocking at the door of her heart, timidly seeking admittance.

Perhaps it would not hurt to allow her in for the evening…

For just this night they would indulge in a fine meal and take advantage of Mr Benton's misplaced courtship. He would never know how relieved she was that the cost had not come from her own purse.

Tonight she would write Mr Benton a note of thanks, and inform him that, since she had no intention of accepting his proposal, the gifts must cease.

She had got her family by on fish and potatoes in the past. She would do so again.

While his gifts were generous, and she would use the kindest words to thank him, she would also be firm in her rejection of his proposal.

Two days later she discovered that it was going to be more difficult than writing a polite letter.

Returning from fetching George from school, Clara found the table set with yet another feast—and their benefactor happily ensconced at the head of the table.

'Mr Benton has agreed to dine with us, Clara,' Lilly announced. 'Isn't that wonderful?'

Wonderful? It was not even acceptable. But what was she to do? What had he done wrong other than being the brother of a thief? Other than trying to make amends, even if in a questionable way?

Admittedly a tempting way…

'Welcome, Mr Benton. And thank you for brining dinner. It is kind of you.'

'Oh, Clara.' Lilly gave a small laugh, her smile happier than it had been in a long time. 'We have gone well past "Mr Benton". We have begun calling him Andrew.'

Oh? Andrew, was it? And how long until her sister had her married off to the man? Or perhaps Lilly had already accepted in her stead?

Andrew had accepted Lilly's invitation to dine with the family knowing that he would only be welcome until her sister returned home and asked him to leave.

Clara Albright puzzled him. He was offering a perfectly respectable way out of the trouble his brother had caused, and yet she was disinclined to accept it.

Firmly disinclined.

No matter. He would persevere in his goal and hope that in time she would accept his help. If anything happened to this good lady, or anyone who belonged to her, he would not be able to live with it.

Miles had ruined her. Andrew would save her. It was only right to do so.

As soon as the door opened and he saw the expression on Mrs Albright's face he realised all over again how big a challenge winning this lady over was going to be. Even remaining at the table throughout this meal would be an accomplishment.

But what Clara did not know about him was that he was a determined man. As determined as he believed her to be.

And what he had on his side was the fact that his cause was a righteous one. For the sake of honour, in the name of decency, he could not fail. Surely the good Lord was on his side?

Also, he had an ally in Lilly. Probably in Annabeth as well. If only cake was all it would take to convince her mother, they should wed.

'Good evening, Mrs Albright,' he said, standing... smiling.

She was a lovely woman. He'd always thought so. No matter if she was smiling or frowning, she was striking. Her wavy red hair and her snapping green eyes were difficult to look away from. It was hard to imagine that four years after her husband's death she remained a widow, even given her circumstances .

Seeming to recover from the surprise of seeing him sitting at her table, she offered a polite smile.

It was Spencer Albright he had associated with. Mrs Albright had used to stand beside her husband, not taking the centre of attention and yet being it, nonetheless. She'd had that presence about her which made everyone else seem... What was it? Dimmer, perhaps?

Seeing her in this moment brought it all back. After all that had happened, all she had endured, she still had a way of wrapping a person up in her smile.

'Welcome,' she said, and then stooped to catch her

daughter in a hug. 'Were you a good girl for your aunt while I was out, my little redbird?'

Redbird must an endearment which had to do with the shade of Annabeth's hair, which was a match to her mother's—except it was bright where Clara's was deep.

'Mr Benton played a game with me.'

'How kind of him. What did you play?'

'Guess the end of the story.'

Children's games were foreign to him. He knew no familiar stories to tell a little girl, so making one up was the best he'd been able to do at short notice. To have her make up the ending had been helpful beyond words.

'That sounds creative.' She set her daughter down, turned her attention back to him. 'Thank you for keeping Annabeth entertained. And, once again, for dinner.'

The five of them sat down to eat. It was not as uncomfortable a meal as it might have been. Although largely that had to do with Lilly keeping up a lively conversation.

The young lady wanted to know about life in Mayfair. About popular fashions for ladies, in particular. It was a subject he was completely ignorant of. Luckily, she did not seem to notice this lack, but chattered happily on.

Perhaps Lilly was simply happy to have someone new to visit. He knew from their earlier conversation, before her sister had got home, that she wished to make a society match, but feared it would be impossible since she had no gowns to attract a suitor.

Her fear was not misplaced. As her life was now, any match with a peer would be unlikely. But with his help it might be. While Andrew was not a peer, he socialised with those who were. It would be no great feat to set Lilly's dream in motion…as long as her sister agreed to marry him. But, while dinner had been pleasant, he did not believe he was making any progress towards winning Clara's hand.

At least he had yet to be shown the door. That was something to be glad of.

When the meal was over, Clara escorted him down the stairs.

It would have been nice to stay and socialise further, but apparently that was not to be.

'May I call upon you again?' he asked.

'Mr Benton, did you not read my note? We are not courting. It is not appropriate for you to call or to leave gifts, as appreciated as they are.'

'You have a lovely family, Mrs Albright. It is my pleasure to—'

'Goodnight, sir.'

She opened the door to the outside steps. He started

down them and then turned back. 'I wonder, would you object to me accompanying you when you bring George home from school tomorrow? He has confided that he is having trouble with a couple of the other boys. Perhaps if they see a man coming to meet him the bullies will leave him alone.'

She had been pulling the door closed, but what he said must have made her reconsider, for she stepped outside. Shut the door behind her.

'What did he say? About the boys who are mistreating him?'

A deep frown wrinkled her brow. He had the most inappropriate urge to smooth it away with the pad of his thumb.

'He says that the boys, two of them, are taller than the others. They are mean to everyone, but it is George they focus their mischief on. These boys brag about how their own fathers are scrappers...boxers who fight behind taverns. They taunt George for being an orphan.'

'He told you all this?' She shook her head, looking a little bewildered.

'He wouldn't want you to worry. Besides, it's easier for a boy to speak with a man about this sort of problem.'

'Did he say he wishes for you to pick him up?'

'I did not offer. Not without your approval. But he

would surely feel much better about going to school if he was not being picked on.'

'You are right, of course. If he had his way George would go to work in his late father's factory. When we...' She glanced past his shoulder and pursed her lips while staring at his coach beside the kerb. 'When we fell on hard times, he was old enough to know the difference between the way we live now and the way we lived then. Georgie has such a good heart...he thinks that he can help by joining the labour force. It is absurd, but I cannot convince him of it.'

'First of all, you did not "fall on hard times". My brother put you there. And as for George going to work—there is no reason he should have to. I have offered you and your family a way out, Mrs Albright. Please consider it.'

'But why have you?'

Her eyes went wide and she gave him an arch look. Even in the dim light of the lantern he saw them turn a more serious shade of green, if such a thing were possible.

'I must make amends for my brother's crime.'

'By offering your life to strangers? May I point out that is not logical?'

'Doing the right thing is often not logical.'

Although in his mind it was perfectly logical. Nothing made more sense than a woman having a husband to watch out for her interests.

'You might simply return the money your brother robbed from me.' She nodded at his carriage. 'I assume you can afford to?'

'I would do so, even if it took all I had, if it was the right thing to do.'

'You do not believe it is?' Her fingers began to tap an impatient rhythm at her waist.

'Naturally not. An unmarried lady with money is vulnerable to any scoundrel's schemes.'

'As it happens, I have learned that lesson.'

He had to blink. It seemed that even the ringlets springing from her hair were snapping with indignation now. The curling ends looked too hot to touch. Not that he would mind touching one to discover if that was true...

'I will never hand over my finances to the care of a man again.'

With a huff, she spun about, opened the front door. 'I bid you goodnight, Mr Benton. It has been a pleasure, I am sure.'

Standing there, gazing up, having been as neatly dismissed as he had ever been, he said, 'About George... Will you allow me to accompany you to retrieve him from school?'

A moment passed, silent except for some mysterious scurrying noises and the unwholesome laughter of night dwellers.

'I shall see you a quarter of an hour before three o'clock. We shall take your carriage, if you do not mind. It will make an impression on those boys.'

'I will see you then.'

Going into the building, she paused in closing the door, leaving a gap through which she peered out at him.

'Goodnight, Andrew,' she said, then clicked the door closed.

All at once he felt like leaping from the middle step to the pavement. It must mean something that she had called him Andrew. Not that she'd agreed to marry him, but at least this was not their last goodbye.

For that much he was grateful.

For that much he held a glimmer of hope.

If she did come round to his way of thinking it would be a stroke of good luck for him as well as her. He could enter a marriage of convenience without risking his heart.

Everyone stood to gain by their union.

Hopefully she would soon see the wisdom of it.

Nothing had ever felt quite so wrong, Clara decided, as being handed up into Andrew's elegant carriage dressed in a patched and faded gown.

The large driver had nodded to her in a proper, decorous way. If she did not look down at what she was wearing she could nearly believe she was the woman she had been four years ago, riding about Mayfair wearing fine brocade.

However, she was not wearing brocade, nor was she enjoying the prosperous streets of Mayfair.

Well, it did not matter, really. She was not the fluffy pampered lady she had once been. She was strong now. Saw the world for what it was. Knew what it took to survive.

The only thing she missed about being that woman was loving Spencer. Her heart had been happy in those days, light in a way it would never be again. But she'd had her one and only love and it would carry her through. The one regret she had was that she and Spencer hadn't had more children. She had miscarried the child she'd been carrying when he died at only eight weeks.

In those days, when sorrow had become too great, she'd focused her love fully on the family she had left. Counting her blessings had helped her heal.

Now, settling on the bench across from Andrew, she glanced outside. Mr Mawbry was watching from his window. Curtains stirred in the attic rooms as well.

Her departure was certainly being noticed.

'Perhaps Lilly and Annabeth would like to ride with us?' Andrew suggested.

Seeing them both, with their noses pressed to the glass, Clara was sorry she had not thought of it herself. Signalling with her fingers, she indicated for them to hurry down.

'It is kind of you to think of them. Thank you, Mr Benton.'

'I thought we had progressed to Andrew?'

'Andrew, then.'

She had called him that last night because she had been so very grateful that he had offered to help George with his problem at school. Boys did need men to guide them. Her stepson was no different.

She studied the man sitting across from her. He looked solid and reliable. Probably not crazy, as she had first assumed. He was handsome too—which had no bearing on his helping George.

Only, to be honest, it had been a long time since she had gazed upon a man with an appreciation for his masculine traits. What a surprise to discover she was enjoying it.

Not that she intended to wed him just because he had compelling eyes that shifted from kind and caring to firm and in charge in the space of a glance.

Nor would she do it because it felt good to be riding safe and high in a carriage, instead of walking, always glancing over her shoulder.

Nor, again, would she wed him because Lilly and Annabeth were beside themselves with joy at being able to take a carriage ride. Truly, Clara had not seen such joy in her sister's eyes since they had been well-to-do and Lilly had had prospects.

There were reasons to wed and there were reasons not to wed.

Mr Andrew Benton held all the reasons not to wed.

She did not know him any more than she knew the man now walking past the carriage and tipping his hat to Lilly.

Andrew Benton was the brother of her enemy.

And he was not Spencer.

Just because she had given up mourning two years ago, it did not mean she wished to marry again.

What she did intend to do was ride to the Ragged School and allow Andrew to make her son feel important. Surely seeing him with a wealthy escort would put those bullies in their place. And perhaps along the way it would do no harm to appreciate Andrew's smile. He did have a well-shaped mouth...

How long had it been since she had felt a man's kiss? Oh, mercy, never mind that! The truth was it had been both too long and not long enough.

Stuff and blather! She would not wed a man to get a kiss!

* * *

The next evening, while riding towards Clara's home, Andrew heard an odd noise. It seemed to be coming from the underside of the carriage, perhaps in the wheel area. It was difficult to know with the sound of rain coming down so hard.

While Clara had made it clear that yesterday's goodbye had been final, Andrew had more to say to young George than he'd had time to yesterday afternoon. While the bullies had been properly wide-eyed at seeing their schoolmate get into a wealthy man's carriage, it did not mean it would be the end of trouble for Clara's stepson. It might be that the show of wealth had offended them, and they would act more aggressively.

Clara was not expecting him. He doubted she would be pleased to see him at her door. But George still needed direction. If he was to remain at school which he clearly ought to, he would need to feel that a man had his back.

The question occupying his mind now, as he jolted along the wet, rutted road, was: between him and the lovely Clara Albright, who was the most determined?

They shared a common goal. To protect her family. How was he to make her see that he was the one with the means to do it? Miles had left her vulnerable. Andrew would keep her secure. The good Lord willing.

That was what he was silently praying when the carriage hit a deep rut, taking a wicked jolt.

Something cracked, the sound sharp and startling. He felt a great thump under the bench, and then found himself sitting on the floor at a cockeyed angle.

Seconds later, the carriage door flew open.

'I am afraid the axle has broken, sir.' Water dripped off the driver's hat and sluiced off his coat. 'We are stuck.'

'So it appears.'

'It is unlikely we will get it repaired tonight.'

The odds of a Hansom cab passing by were slim. No one was out in this weather—especially in this part of town.

It would be a cold, miserable walk home…unless he and the driver spent the night stuffed into the off-kilter cab. But he was far closer to the Albrights' home than Mayfair, and he did have gifts for the children to deliver.

'There is nothing for it but to walk the rest of the way to Mrs Albright's.' He reached under the seat to retrieve the spare raincoat and the box of gifts. 'Hopefully she will put us up for the night. It would not be safe to walk these streets in the dark.'

'You go, Mr Benton. I will not leave the carriage unattended in this area. There might be nothing left of it by morning.'

Hinton was right—and yet it would not be a comfortable night for him, sheltering in a broken carriage.

'I will manage.' He nodded with a grin.

'Watch for me to join you in a few hours.'

'Hopefully the lady will take pity on you and ask you to stay.'

Perhaps… But there was every chance he would be joining Hinton in the carriage.

Running down the three streets to Clara's home, he watched the dark doorways and alleys. Pelting rain notwithstanding, these streets were not safe. He imagined eyes staring at his back the whole way.

But he understood something in a way he had not done before. As impoverished as Clara's home was, to her and her family it was a sanctuary. Giving it up for the unknown future he offered would be hard to do.

He only hoped she might offer him a corner of her sanctuary for the night.

When the knock pounded on the door, no one stared at it in dread.

No one but Clara.

It would be Andrew, of course, coming once again to try and convince her that they should wed.

She would not mind so much if she was not beginning to understand the benefits to her family.

But, no. While many women did marry to improve

their station or their finances, Clara Albright would not be one of them.

The rest of her family would be over the moon to see their visitor, but she was going to turn him away before he set one foot into her home.

The children were getting far too attached to the man as it was.

Lilly opened the door without verifying who it was. But, really, by now they recognised his knock. *Rap-rap.* Pause. *Rap-rap-rap.*

And there he stood, water dripping off his raincoat and hat, a large wooden crate in his arms.

Everyone was smiling. She nearly was too. Because he was beginning to grow on her.

His grin was engaging. The fact could hardly be ignored. However, returning his smile, as everyone else was doing, would not be wise. He would think she was welcoming him, when what she meant was to send him on his way.

Calling on her well-honed frown, she pinned him with it.

But Annabeth took Andrew's gloved hand and drew him into the room. This would not do at all. And now her sister was taking his hat and raincoat.

Sending him on his way was becoming complicated. Nevertheless, she must do it. She could not continue to allow him to call. He would be thinking she was considering his mad proposal.

And not even mad in the normal sense—it was outrageously mad.

'I come bearing gifts.' He set the box on the floor.

Lilly placed his dripping coat outside in the corridor.

Gifts, he called them? Bribes, more like.

For the life of her she could not understand why marrying her was so important to him. No one could feel this repentant for a crime committed by someone else.

'And I must throw myself on your mercy, Clara.'

'A gift for me?' Annabeth asked, sending the conversation another way.

Her daughter hopped about in excitement. Gifts were a rare thing in this household. A small treat for one's birthday was all they amounted to.

Whatever gifts Andrew had brought were bound to be wet. The box was quite soaked for having only made the trip from his carriage and up the front steps. So was he soaked, as far as that went...

'Why must you throw yourself on my mercy?' she asked, while Andrew rooted about in the box.

'Well, you see—'

Annabeth screeched when a doll emerged from the box, with pretty red ringlets and a blue satin ball gown.

Oh, what a pickle Clara was in. She could not accept such an extravagant gift any more than she could refuse it. Annabeth would be crushed if Clara prised it from her arms—which might be impossible anyway.

She gave the box a stern frown. What other extravagance would come out of it?

To Lilly's clear delight, there was hatpin with pearls. Then for George a sailboat.

With the weather the way it was, George could probably dash outside and send it sailing down the gutter. Not that she would allow that.

In the excitement of gift-giving, Andrew seemed to have forgotten he had told her he must throw himself on her mercy.

'Why is it that you require my mercy?'

The sooner she knew the reason, the sooner she could send him out to his lovely carriage and back to the place where he belonged. And the sooner he would leave her in peace, here in the place where she now belonged.

'Ah… The axle on my carriage broke on the way here. I find myself stranded.'

'Then you must spend the night with us!' Lilly said, while admiring her pearly pin in the lamplight and then attaching it to her collar. 'Mustn't he, Clara?'

'I do not expect that, of course,' he said. 'But if you will allow me to warm by the fire until I dry, I will spend the night in the carriage with my driver.'

He would once again be soaked to the bone by the time he arrived at the carriage. To turn him onto the streets in a storm would be unconscionable. She knew what it was to be turned out. To do it to someone even for one night? No, she simply could not.

Besides, there was no one to judge it improper for her to allow him to spend the night in her home. Society had quite forgotten her. And with Lilly and the children as chaperons, his presence would be respectable. Allowing the man shelter was the only honourable thing to do.

Relenting, she said, 'You have arrived in time for dinner. And of course you will stay the night with us.'

Even though dinner was only what had been left over from what he had brought last time, her family would consider it a feast.

It occurred to her that the fish seller must be wondering what had become of her. She had not visited his stall in more than a week...

Even though she would not have chosen to have Andrew stranded in her home, here he was. She might as well make the best of it, the same way the rest of her family was doing. She might even enjoy his company had he not proposed marriage and made her feel on edge over it.

Watching him through the meal, she had no sense that *he* felt on edge over anything. He laughed and chatted happily, as if he were simply a family friend and not someone seeking a spot as head of that family.

After dinner, Andrew took George aside for a man-to-man talk. No doubt it had to do with the bullies, and how to carry on with them in the future. Hopefully it was good advice, since Andrew would no longer be picking George up in his elegant, if now disabled carriage.

A thought flitted through her mind. Where would George attend school if she married Andrew? Probably somewhere prestigious, as he would have done had his father lived. And had Miles Holmes not stolen her money.

Apparently finished with their talk, the 'men' joined the ladies in front of the fireplace. The last thing Clara wished was to feel sweetly fuzzy while watching the pair of them. But there was no getting around the fact that Andrew was standing in the place George's late father would have. Perhaps it was only for a moment, but even so her heart went soft.

Andrew had no sooner settled in his chair than Lilly said, 'We should dance!'

She spun about in her plain brown skirt, arms wide. No doubt her sister was imagining her gown to be satin and lace, sparkling in the light of a dozen chandeliers.

Lilly had a happy imagination.

She extended her hand to Andrew. 'My only partner has been my sister. Practising with an actual gentleman would be so helpful.'

Andrew rose. Bowed. 'Miss Lilly, may I have the pleasure of a waltz about the ballroom?'

The 'ballroom' being her small parlour, with a table and two chairs to get in the way.

Lilly did not seem a bit troubled by the cramped space.

'Clara, will you hum the music?' her sister asked.

'We shall all hum.' She liked humming, but she did not wish to be the only one doing it.

It was the oddest sound…

Annabeth's young voice, George's boyish one and Andrew's deep, manly one, blending with hers and Lilly's.

Nice, though. One might nearly imagine they were a happy family spending a contented evening together.

One might… However it might not be the wisest thing to do. She had no more inkling of what Andrew required in a family and marriage than he had of what she required. There had been no discussion of it before he'd asked for her hand.

The proposal had come out of the blue. No woman with a penny's worth of common sense would accept it. Or was it the other way around? Any woman in her situation with any common sense *would* accept it?

After a few moments, Lilly drew Andrew over to Clara and placed her fingers in his hand in a change of partners. It was impossible to determine which of them was more surprised to find themselves touching the other. His brows arched and she felt herself blushing.

Andrew recovered first. 'May I have the pleasure of this dance, Mrs Albright?' He bowed over her hand, a proper gentleman.

Not completely against her will, she nodded. This was all in fun—she understood that. And yet that understanding did not prevent echoes of the past from tickling her heart. Did not keep her from swaying ever so slightly in time with the hum her family was making.

She'd used to adore dancing, once upon a time...

Andrew's hand pressed into her back. His hand was large, with long fingers which warmed the back of her gown. Having not been touched by a man in more than four years she felt... What? Wrong? Right? Joyful...bitter?

All of those things.

Unsure whether to smile or cry, she decided to laugh. It was the reaction best in keeping with the cheerful mood Lilly was striving to create.

'You are a skilled dancer, Andrew,' she told him. 'You must get a lot of practice.'

'I cannot remember the last time I indulged in this particular pleasure.'

'Truly? I cannot either,' she admitted. 'I suppose dancing is something one does forget easily.'

'Our skill might have to do with the music.' He glanced at her family, merrily humming, and grinned. 'I cannot say I have heard finer.'

'My turn!' Annabeth cried.

Pushing between them, her daughter looked up at Andrew, her expression bright and expectant.

Andrew took her daughter's small hand, bowed low over it. 'May I have the pleasure of this dance, Miss Redbird? I hope I may call you that?'

'Yes, sir.' And she stood on his feet, danced on top of his stockings.

It seemed the oddest thing to be looking at a near-stranger's striped socks. But with his shoes drying in front of the fireplace there they were. She could hardly avoid seeing the outline of his long toes pressing against the weave.

Had they actually been a family, and not just playing the part for an evening, it would not be strange to see his socks, or even his bare feet.

While she enjoyed watching her daughter's pleasure, she kept in mind that this was only a moment out of time, forced upon them by the weather and a broken carriage. The five of them were not a family, for all it seemed like it.

After their voices grew hoarse from humming, the dancing ended. Andrew added some coals to the fire, and they all gathered around the hearth for warmth.

What a cosy scene it was. Andrew in the chair beside hers, Lilly seated upon a cushion on the floor with George's head cradled on her lap. Annabeth was already asleep in Andrew's arms, looking quite content.

Lilly was asking Andrew dozens of questions. Which of her former friends had made proper matches? Who remained unmarried and who had hosted the most spoken-of ball?

Andrew said that, not being a part of society, he did not really know, but still Lilly hung on his every word.

In time George fell asleep, with his arms curled around his new boat and his soft snores ruffling his aunt's skirt. And when at last Lilly seemed to run out of questions, she scooted out from under him. She took her niece from Andrew's arms and carried her into the bedroom they shared.

'I'll take George,' Andrew said, then picked him and the boat up, carried them to his cot in the kitchen.

Beside Clara's chair there was a basket of sewing beside which held her newest commission. She reached for it, not able to fully repress a weary sigh. Just because she had entertained an unexpected guest this evening did not change the fact that she needed to earn a living.

'Is there something I can do to help?' Andrew asked, taking his place once more in the other chair. 'As you are stuck with me, you might as well put me to use.'

'I do not suppose you know how to stich beads onto lace?'

He shook his head. A hank of hair, golden brown in the glow of the flames, fell across his brow. He stretched his legs, wriggled his striped socks in the warmth.

'I wonder if my shoes are dry. I suppose I ought to put them back on.'

'Do not bother. There is nothing quite as nice as warming one's toes on a chilly night. In fact, I shall do the same.'

With her shoe halfway off, she remembered that both toes of her stockings were patched and mended. Too late to hide it now, so she set her shoes aside. She refused to be ashamed. She would enjoy the warmth on her toes.

'We have a love of warm feet in common, at least,' Andrew commented.

Perhaps... But many people loved that. However, even if they were the only ones in London who did, that bond was not reason enough to wed, to give their futures to one another.

Even though she was not going to give him her hand, she wanted to know why he was so willing to offer his. He had told her, of course, but quite honestly it made no sense.

'Why do you wish to marry me?' she asked. 'Do not tell me it is because you want to make up for what your brother did. That is illogical. If it is an act of charity you wish to perform, there are poor widows aplenty in London who would welcome your help.'

'Yes, but as far as I know it was not my brother who plunged them into poverty.' He leaned forward, elbows on his knees, and looked her steadily in the eye. 'What you must be wondering is what do I gain by our marriage besides easing my conscience?'

'Yes, indeed—that is what I want to know. I no longer believe you are insane, the way I did when you first proposed. And if you are not, then you must hope to gain something for handing over your future to me and my family. No one is that altruistic.'

She gave her attention back to the beads. The client was expecting her gown to be finished three days from now.

'I might be. My father was a minister, you see.'

She did not see. Ministers' children went astray as often as anyone else's children did.

'I cut my teeth on the Good Book and on my father's strong sense of right and wrong,' he told her.

'He died doing good for the poor. It only makes sense that I should feel responsible for you and your family. But you are correct about there being more to it.'

'That part where it benefits you?'

She set her sewing on her lap, pinned her needle to her collar. This was far too interesting a conversation to give it only half her attention.

'Our marriage would benefit my mother.' He rubbed his palms together, a gesture which made him look nervous. 'She is frail...emotionally. I fear that she will become mortally depressed if she discovers what her youngest child is. She has always doted upon my brother, and if she discovers what he did to you she might not recover.'

'I'm sorry, Andrew. But I do not understand how marrying me helps with that.'

'If you marry me you will no longer be ruined. In the event Mother does discover the truth, the crime will already be put to rights. I know this makes little sense to you. My brother did what he did, and that cannot be changed. But if Mother sees you are not destroyed by it, it will ease her distress.'

'I am not destroyed.'

She might not be the sparkling innocent she had been, but she was not destroyed—far from it. What she was, was independent, and that was how she meant to stay, thank you very much.

'As you can see.'

Hopefully he was not looking at the patched toes of her stockings, nor noticing how damp the room felt in the rain, or he might not believe her.

'Who, may I ask, is providing shelter to whom tonight?'

'I take your point, Clara.'

'What I would like to know is why you have not already wed. Surely many ladies must have been wishing for your proposal.'

'I have not felt any urgency to wed until now, nor the desire to do so.'

'And suddenly you do?'

'Yes, suddenly there is a need. You and your family must be protected.'

'First of all, I do not need a man to watch over me and my money. I have learned to do perfectly well on my own.' She picked up the sewing in her lap. 'Surely there is a woman you fancy in a romantic way? And if you do not now, you will one day. I do not wish to be the burden that stands between you and your one true love.'

'That sounds rather dramatic, Clara. You need not fear that will happen. What you *should* fear is something unfortunate happening and you facing it alone.'

'Something more unfortunate than losing my husband? Something worse than being turned out on the streets with small children?'

He must not have any answer, because he stared at her mended stockings in utter silence.

'I have made my own security, Andrew. I will not hand it over to you.'

And that was all she had to say.

'I believe I respect you more than any woman I have ever met,' he murmured. 'Please say you will marry me.'

Very well, she might have one more thing to say.

'No, I will not.'

Chapter Four

Three days later, the last thing Andrew expected was to find a messenger at his door with a note from Clara.

The writing was not neat and appeared to be scribbled in haste. He had to take it to the window for added light to read what it said.

It took him three reads to be certain he was seeing it right.

At a run, he summoned the carriage to be brought round without delay.

Jones had barely handed him his coat and hat before he'd rushed out the front door.

He did not wait for his driver to step down and open the carriage door.

'George is missing,' he called up. 'Mrs Albright is asking for help.'

The door had not even closed before the coach lurched into motion.

This was not an appropriate speed for crowded

streets, but George was missing. He did not tell the driver to slow down. It would be dark before long. Already the afternoon shadows stretched long and the air was cooling.

The carriage had not fully come to a stop at Clara's home before he leapt out, dashed up the steps.

Clara stood at the top of the stairs, her hands clutched at her waist. She pressed her lips together, but still they trembled at the corners.

Without thinking he wrapped her in his arms, held her. 'Don't be afraid. I'm here now. I will find him.'

'I took him to school, as I always do. I saw him go inside…'

A shiver ran through her. It crept though Andrew too.

'He wasn't there when I returned to collect him.'

'Let's go, then.' He snatched her hand, hurried her down the stairs. 'Is Lilly with Annabeth?'

'I told her to stay here in case George comes home.'

'Where have you looked?'

'Around the school,' she said, as he handed her up into the carriage. 'I thought we would make better time in your carriage, and he might notice us looking for him.'

'You did right to send for me. Have you spoken with the teachers?'

She nodded. 'They said he had claimed to be feeling unwell and was going home. Which he did not do.'

'And he was feeling well this morning?'

'Perfectly well. I have never let him walk alone... These streets...' Tears stood at the corners of this brave woman's eyes. 'You don't think...?'

'No, I do not. He is a clever lad.'

'And only ten years old! He will be kidnapped by—'

'No, Clara.' He took her chin between his fingers and tried to give her courage with a nod, and as confident a gaze as he could manage. 'I think I know where he is.'

He hoped he knew—because if he was wrong it would be a perilous night for George. He would have Hinton drive the carriage around all night long, if need be, looking for him, but he thought perhaps he was right about where the boy had gone.

'Where?' Clara wiped the back of her hand across her cheek.

'To his father's factory.'

He thumped on the roof. The carriage stopped. Seconds later Hinton opened the door and Andrew instructed the driver where to go.

'But he wouldn't,' said Clara. 'I've made it clear that he must remain in school.'

'And yet he sees how hard you work to take care of

them all. Don't you see, Clara? In his eyes he is nearly grown and he should be contributing.'

'He would not go against what I wish. Georgie is a good boy.'

'He is. And that is why I think he has gone to the one place where he believes he can help. It stands to reason he would go there.'

It was nearly dark when they reached the factory. Long shadows fell across the vendors' stalls nearby, which were mostly closed up for the night.

Getting out of the carriage, Clara ran ahead of him to the door where the employees would exit. The door was locked. She pounded hard, but there was no answer.

'Let's have a look around,' said Andrew. 'Maybe he's here. Perhaps hiding. I imagine he knows by now he is in trouble.'

'I hope he is here. Otherwise he is in another sort of trouble which... Oh, Andrew, I cannot even think about it.'

'Do not think it. Not for a moment.'

They circled the outside of the building without finding him. Twilight was coming on fast with all the tall buildings around. Now Andrew admitted to feeling a bit of fear. Admitted it to himself.

To Clara he offered expressions of confidence.

'Unless I miss my guess, our boy is on his way

home now, shaking in his shoes at the thought of having to face you.'

Silently, he sent up a prayer that this was true. And if it was not that an angel would be following George's every step.

Judging by the look on Clara's face, the boy might need that angel, even if he was at this moment safe at home.

Clara felt as if her heart was walking on the dark streets, naked and helpless.

Oh, she'd tried to be reasonable and believe what Andrew said, about George being on his way home, probably shaking in his shoes with worry over being punished.

Fear, however, was stronger than reason. And it suggested that the child had been snatched from the earth…that she would never see him again and it was all her fault.

She wanted to scream, to weep and cry. To open the carriage door and be sick on the road.

'You look out of one window,' Andrew said. 'I will look out of the other. We are bound to see him.'

She nodded, too agitated to speak because of what she could see through the window.

A ragged-looking man crept from doorway to doorway. Why was he doing that? Looking for a vulnerable child to take…? To sell into…?

All of a sudden she felt the carriage shift, then Andrew's large, firm hand wrapped around hers and squeezed.

'My driver has an excellent view. We will find him. You must believe me.'

'I am doing my best, but I have never lost a child before.'

'You have not lost one now, either. George made the decision to do what you had forbidden him to.'

'Thank you for reminding me of that. While I am looking for him I shall think of how to discipline him. After I finish hugging the life out of him.'

Although it was growing dim inside the carriage, she saw Andrew smile. That simple gesture gave her more comfort than she would ever have guessed.

'Did you ever run away as a child, Andrew?'

'I did not dare. As the son of a minister, I'd have had to sit through a half-day sermon if I had. Wasn't worth it.'

'I ran away once.'

'I see you survived it. So will George. But why did you?'

'To get married. My parents did not approve of Spencer because he was not a peer.'

'That was unfair,' he said, glancing briefly away

from his view of the street. 'Your husband was a good man—a worthy one.'

Andrew returned his attention to his window. After only a moment, he looked back at her, grinned. 'I see our boy.'

The carriage had slowed while he was speaking. The driver must have spotted George as well.

This was the second time Andrew had referred to George as their boy. In the moment she did not correct him, because she did not know what she would have done without his help.

'Oh, just wait until I get my hands on that child!'

Andrew opened the door. 'Let me get him.'

'Oh, no. I am his mother, and I must—'

'You are, of course. But Clara, you must understand—he no longer sees himself as a boy. In his eyes he is a man. And he means to stand in his father's place.'

'He shall soon discover his mistake,' she said, getting out of the carriage. 'But I would not take it amiss if you came with me Andrew.'

It was dark. How far away was that lurking man? What was to say there was not someone else like that out there? A come-hither strumpet, perhaps, set on stealing a young boy's virtue?

Stepping out, Andrew offered a hand to help her down. It was a good, strong hand. No matter how independent she knew herself to be, she was glad to be holding on to it.

'Don't forget to hug him first,' Andrew said.

Lilly opened the door while they were still coming up the stairs. She dabbed at her eyes with her apron. Given how red and swollen her eyes were, Clara knew she must have been weeping ever since she and Andrew had gone looking for George.

With her hand clamped lightly on George's shoulder, Clara felt it when he jerked. Seeing his aunt in this condition might be all the reprimand the boy needed. And a boy he was—Andrew's opinion that he was changing into a man notwithstanding.

She was about to point out his aunt's tears as an illustration that he could not simply do what he wished. That his actions had repercussions on other people. And she would have. But George had dashed the rest of the way up the stairs, wrapped his arms around Lilly and begun weeping, too.

Andrew remained for a few moments, but then bade them good evening and left them to sort things out as a family.

'I do not know what to do with you, George,' said Clara. 'Why would you do this to us?'

'Lilly wants a gown,' he stated between hiccups.

'Georgie…' Clara went down on her knees and

hugged him tight. It was odd, she suddenly realised, that she had to look up at him in that position. When had that happened? 'It is not for you to get your aunt a gown.'

'I am almost ready to turn into a man.'

Clara stood, tipped his face up to hers. That was more comfortable. She could hardly convince him he was not a man when she had to look up to him.

'My father would have bought her a gown. I must do it since he cannot.'

The reminder of their loss hit her as hard as a physical blow. The force of what he'd said took the breath out of her for a moment.

She had done her best to provide everything they needed. Not in a luxurious way, but they were not starving or living in an alley.

'What did you think, son? That I would believe you were at school when you were at the factory, throwing away your childhood?'

'Georgie,' Lilly said. 'I do not need a gown that badly. Promise me you will not do that again.'

'I... I promise.' Her sweet, tearful son wiped his nose on his sleeve. 'But Lilly, if you marry Mr Benton he will buy you a gown.'

Clara ruffled Georgie's hair, so grateful he was safely at home.

'Lilly will have far more than a gown when she

eventually marries,' Clara explained. 'She will have a husband who adores her. A lady should not marry without love.'

'Andrew loves us,' Annabeth declared. 'We know it, Mama.'

'He is a good man.' She could not say otherwise. 'We will always remember his kindness to us.'

'Drink your tea, my boy, before it grows cold. And have a sandwich.' Andrew's mother extended the dainty cucumber sandwiches towards him. 'You would not wish to hurt Cook's feelings.'

He took a sandwich, ate it in one bite.

'Oh, good. You have an appetite after all. With how distracted you seem, I am surprised that you do.'

'I'm sorry, Mother. I am preoccupied by a business matter.'

The business of winning a wife and a family.

He was more convinced than ever that the Albrights needed him. The problem was, the more convinced he became, the less inclined Clara seemed to accept his proposal.

He'd been awake all night, thinking over what she'd said about returning the money his brother had taken. It was not as if he could not afford to. His business was profitable.

But after wrestling with the idea until sunrise poked

through his chamber window, he had decided he could not. The poor houses he'd used to visit with his father were reminder enough that a woman alone was easily cheated. While settling with his brother's victim financially would be the easiest solution, he could not in good conscience do it.

And besides all that, Clara Albright was not simply his brother's victim any longer. The realisation had become quite clear days ago. He liked Clara and her family. He enjoyed their company.

He missed them.

After not seeing them for two weeks, he felt the loss. Although at the same time he thought it might be best to wait for Clara to offer an invitation for him to visit, perhaps share a meal with them as he had done that night he'd spent asleep in her worn chair.

He had been pressing his suit before, but now he felt it best to give her time to think it over…perhaps miss him a bit too.

If a man needed to wed, he was not sorry to have proposed to a woman as fine as Clara. And while he waited, not very patiently, he wondered what was going on in her poor but cosy home.

Had George gone obediently back to school? He had sent over several boxes of food, so they were probably not hungry…

'You spend far too much time on business matters, Andrew.'

His mother poked another sandwich at him. He took it, held the dainty thing in two fingers, then popped it into his mouth.

'What you need is a wife to distract you from your numbers. It is time and past that you married.'

It was fascinating how one's mother could see into one's soul.

'It would make you happy if I did?' he asked.

'But of course! You and your brother both need to marry. Please make me a grandmother before I am too doddering to enjoy my grandchildren.'

Footsteps came past the dining room and moved down the corridor. The sound of the butler's voice drifted up from the hall.

'That must be your brother at long last. I have not seen him in so long. If only he would find a respectable lady to settle down with…'

'Oh, well, you know Miles, Mother. He is probably spending a great deal of time at his club.'

All of his time…given that his current 'club' was prison.

Jones stepped into the small parlour. 'Mr Benton, there is a visitor asking to see you. She claims she does not have an appointment, but insists it is urgent.'

She? There was only one lady who might call on him, but surely it could not be—?

'Did she give you her name?'

'Miss Lilly Albright. The young lady appears distraught, if I might say so, sir.'

'Excuse me, Mother.'

She would wonder why he'd rushed out so suddenly without explaining why a distraught young lady should come seeking him.

Had Lilly come all this way on foot?

If George had run away again Andrew would have a stern word with the boy, no matter if Clara thought he was overstepping bounds.

Blight it, he thought, while rushing to the hall. He could not imagine what would bring Lilly here unless it was something desperate.

At his first sight of her, pale and winded, with a fireplace poker gripped in her fist, he knew it was.

'What is wrong?'

He indicated that Jones should bring Lilly a chair, but she waved it away.

'It's Annabeth,' she gasped. 'She is terribly sick. Please help us, Andrew.'

Before asking what the child's trouble was, he called for the carriage to be brought around. Next he sent a message with a swift, young footman to his mother's physician, advising him that he would collect him within the half-hour. Hopefully the doctor was at home and would be willing to accompany Andrew at such sudden notice.

With a wave of his hand he indicated that Lilly should follow him to the carriage house. He would discover exactly what the trouble was once they were on their way.

Clara was a level-headed woman and not prone to overreaction. Whatever was wrong, it must be dire. So urgent that she'd sent Lilly out alone.

When Annabeth had grown ill, with every symptom it seemed a child could get, Clara had not known what to do.

Everything she'd tried to do to help had failed. Each time she'd thought she'd managed to get Annabeth's fever down it had come raging back, worse than before. Every time she'd got a mouthful of broth down her daughter's throat it had come back up.

It had been when Annabeth sat up on the bed and pointed to the monkeys she saw frolicking on the walls that Clara had done the one thing left to do.

The thing she ought to have done first.

She sent for Andrew.

Two days ago, when Annabeth had first become ill, her immediate instinct had been to send for him. But she'd told herself she could not continue to call on him for every problem that arose. It was not as if he was her husband.

And, having managed many childhood ailments over the years, she'd had no reason to believe she could not handle this one as well.

That had been a couple of long days ago...before the monkeys.

When creatures seen only by Annabeth had clawed up Clara's apron and made her sick child screech, there had been nothing for it but to call upon the one person she knew she could count upon.

The only person she could count on.

Oh, she'd cursed herself aplenty for not having sent for Andrew sooner. It was pride that had kept her from it, she knew. Pride and her cherished self-sufficiency.

Because how was she to call herself an independent woman and yet turn to Andrew Benton at every turn?

But this day had illustrated to her that there were times in life when depending upon one's self and no one else was not the wisest path.

It had been late afternoon when Clara had done the unthinkable. She'd sent Lilly out alone, armed with only a fireplace poker and a prayer.

How long would it take her to get to him? Too long, is what, when every second seemed an hour. As long as Lilly encountered no mishap she ought to make it before sundown. It made all the difference, daylight or twilight. Once she was with Andrew she would be safe but…

Oh, curse these long moments of waiting. Of sitting helplessly by and watching Annabeth's laboured breathing…all the while wondering if her sister made it safely to Andrew.

How many times could she count herself a fool for not summoning Andrew yesterday? She knew, of course. A dozen times in the past two hours alone— one for each time Annabeth had moaned in fitful sleep.

Surely it must be possible for a woman to be confident in her abilities and at the same time rely on a man for help?

But sitting here she was not confident…she was terrified.

How foolish, how vain of her, to believe she was in control of everything that happened to her family. The last few hours had illustrated quite vividly that she was not. The last couple of weeks, too, if she cared to look back to George running away.

Had it not been for Andrew, anything might have happened to her boy. Not that she had given him the appreciation he deserved. She had been distracted by getting George home and how she would deal with his disobedience. She feared she had all but dismissed Andrew without proper thanks.

Who would blame him if he did not come? Time and again he had offered her a way out of the precarious way they lived. And she had spurned his proposal of marriage at every turn.

After rescuing George, Andrew had deserved to be sent away with a great hug of thanks, perhaps even a kiss on the cheek. What he had got was a distracted thank-you followed by two long weeks of no communication of any kind. From her at least. Andrew had continued to send food, bless the man.

Still, when it came to illness there was no guarantee that he would be able to help. Andrew might not be able to do more than she had already done. The plain fact was she did not wish to be alone.

She might have asked Mr Mawbry to come. Together she and her neighbour might have stood over Annabeth's bed, wringing their hands.

But she had sent for Andrew. Because… Well, because he would not wring his hands. He would use them to help in whatever way he could.

Hearing carriage wheels on the street, slowing then coming to a stop, she dashed to the window. Andrew! How could she have doubted that he would come?

Before the driver could step down, he'd bounded out of the carriage, followed by Lilly and a man carrying a black bag.

Could Andrew have brought a doctor with him?

Of course he had.

Andrew Benton always knew what to do.

Simply hearing his footsteps pounding up the stairs, she felt a great weight lift off her shoulders...off her soul. She was no longer alone in this emergency.

There would be the matter of paying the doctor. She would not manage to do it. However, if she knew Andrew at all—and she was beginning to feel she did—he would cover the cost.

She would reimburse him somehow... But that was a thought for another time.

"Lilly!" Clara rushed to her sister, wrapped her in a great, relieved hug. "Thank the Good Lord you made it safe."

Seeing Andrew kneeling side by side with the doctor, next to the bed, and his genuine concern for her daughter, she had to wonder how Andrew and Miles could be so different from one another. It made no sense that one brother should be trustworthy and the other without virtue.

Annabeth must have sensed Andrew's presence, because she opened her eyes and smiled weakly at him. Then she reached a pale slender hand towards him. Andrew held it to his cheek, kissed her fingertips.

Then Annabeth frowned at the doctor. 'There were monkeys on the wall,' she told him.

'I didn't see them!' George cried, seeming disappointed that he had not.

'Those were special monkeys,' the doctor explained. 'Not everyone sees them. They come to make sick little children laugh.'

Clara wished she had thought to say such a thing. In that moment they could have done with a laugh. But all she had been was frightened witless.

'I imagine they have gone now?' the doctor asked Annabeth.

'Yes, sir.'

'That is good.' He glanced at Clara over his shoulder, gave her a nod. 'There is something I know about those special monkeys. When they go away they leave behind healing dust. It sparkles down all over sick little girls and makes them feel better. I bet your mother saw it.'

'Oh, yes. It was so pretty, Annabeth,' Clara said. 'You had your eyes closed, or you would have seen it too.'

'I saw it too, Bethie,' George declared. 'Not the monkeys, I didn't see them, but the dust looked like magic twinkles.'

If Annabeth had wanted to question the truth of magic dust, she probably no longer did. If her big brother claimed to believe it, she would believe it too.

Andrew stood up. He went to the parlour window and took one of the two chairs and put it beside the bed.

The doctor sat down and settled his weight, giving the impression that he would be there for a long time.

Magic monkey dust…if only it were true. But if her daughter slept more peacefully believing in it, then there was magic going on inside her.

Andrew took Clara's hand, led her out to the corridor.

'We are going to need more chairs. I'll send my driver to get some.'

He turned to go downstairs and speak with Hinton.

Clara caught his arm when he was one step down. His bicep was firm, so strong and reliable under her fingertips.

'Andrew, are you always in control of situations? It seems to me you never fail to know what needs to be done, no matter what is going on.'

'I suppose I am.' He gave her a questioning look, the slightest lift of a brow. 'Does it bother you? Me taking over?'

'Not as much as it used to.'

She let go of his arm, only now realising she was still clinging to it. Odd, that. His arm being so strong and manly, she ought to have been keenly aware of touching him…

'Are you shivering, Clara?'

Was she? Probably. Since she had been trembling on the inside ever since she'd sent her sister running for help.

Now that help was here, she let the tension go.

Andrew stepped up to her level, wrapped one arm around her shoulders and pressed her head to his chest with the other.

'Don't worry...' He rocked her ever so slightly as he spoke. 'Everything will be all right. Wait and see.'

It would be, she thought, listening to the steady thump of his heart. Standing on the creaky boards in the dim staircase, she felt safe.

How long had it been since she'd simply fallen into a man's arms? Felt the strength of those arms supporting her?

So long that it felt like for ever, not four years.

Perhaps she should not indulge in this particular kind of solace, but at that moment it felt natural. She needed a friend, and this man was so reliable.

'Will you stay the night, Andrew?' she asked. The thought of going through another night fighting an invisible enemy was daunting.

'That was my intention in bringing more chairs. If I am to pace and worry I would rather do it here, where I will not imagine dire things happening out of my sight. Not that dire things are going to happen, Clara. It's only what I would imagine.'

With a nod, he stepped away from her, smiled, then took another step down.

'I'm glad you will be here. Thank you, Andrew.'

He gave her a wink! And in spite of all she was going through, that gesture made her smile.

It was very good not to be alone.

'We will need food,' he said. 'I'll have Hinton ask Cook to send some.'

In control, indeed. More and more, she found she did not mind.

When the chairs arrived, Dr Turner was given the best one, as was fitting. Then Andrew insisted that Clara sit in the chair he'd had brought over from his own chamber. It was fitting for her to have a good chair as well. Any mother who had been through what she had during a long night needed a decent, comfortable place to rest.

Also, he could not deny that seeing her snuggled in the chair he himself used made him feel good. The way her head was rolled back on the cushions now, while she slept, exposed the slender column of her neck and made him feel soft inside.

Why was that? Perhaps it was because she looked delicate but was quite strong. Such a combination was attractive.

But he would think about his feelings later. Right

at this moment he decided the doctor could probably use another cup of coffee. The man had not slept, due to Annabeth's fever going up and down all night long.

Andrew had not slept either, having been kept busy bringing wet towels and making sure coffee was always warming.

Rising from the chair beside Clara's, he took care not to wake her. He went to the kitchen and poured two cups of coffee.

A glance at his timepiece told him that the sun would be rising soon.

Annabeth appeared to be sleeping more peacefully.

Handing one cup to the doctor, he went to stand beside the window. He drew the curtain aside a few inches. Dawn was just beginning to turn the sky pink. Rays of sunshine were yet to poke above tall buildings in the east.

Looking down, he wished Clara and her family did not live in this neighbourhood. There was no longer any reason for them to. This morning the streets were quiet, with respectable vendors beginning to go about their business. Last night that had not been the case. He'd heard all sorts of unsavoury noises going on down below.

Hinton would have heard it too. Although the driver had been dismissed for the evening, he had remained below in the carriage, in the event that he was needed.

Dropping the curtain, Andrew looked down at Clara. Her hair had come undone during the night and it fell over one shoulder. There were dark circles under her eyes, which was understandable. It might be his imagination, but she seemed slimmer than when he had seen her a couple of weeks ago.

In the basket beside the chair lay the pearly gown she had been working on. Hadn't she told him it was meant to be finished…quite a while ago, he thought.

A runaway son and a sick daughter…how thinly could a woman stretch herself? What would be left of Clara, when she needed to be everything for everyone?

It frustrated him. Because it did not need to be this way. She had a way out which she refused to accept. A perfectly respectable way out. He might not be a husband infatuated with his wife, but he would treat her well. Make certain she was comfortable and safe.

It took another second of watching the fine creases drag at the corners of her mouth to make him feel guilty for thinking that way. Her negative attitude about committing her future to any man was the result of what his brother had done to her.

As far as Andrew was concerned, Miles's eleven-month sentence was far too short. His victims would pay the price for far longer than that.

The Clara Albright asleep in that chair was not the same woman he'd met that night of the opera. She was stronger. He admired her more now than he had then. While being forced to live in a bad area of town, Clara had somehow managed to keep her family fed and safe. How many women could go through what she had and come out on top of trouble?

While he was looking at her, not bothering to hide his admiration, she opened her eyes. She gazed softly up at him for a moment, smiled even more softly.

Then all at once her eyes flew wide. She jerked up in the chair, rose, and hurried over to where the doctor was bent over Annabeth, listening to her breathe.

'How is she?' Clara reached down, stroked a strand of damp hair from her daughter's temple.

'It seems the monkey dust is doing its work.'

If Andrew had ever seen anything more welcome than the doctor's grin, he could not recall what it was.

He crossed the room to stand beside Clara, then placed his hand on her shoulder. It was a companionable gesture, and not out of line to his way of thinking. After that moment on the stairs when she had allowed him to hold and comfort her, it did not seem improper to touch her this way.

She reached up, gave his fingers a squeeze.

Good, then. He had not misjudged the moment.

'By this time tomorrow I expect her to be much recovered,' the doctor announced.

He felt Clara sag in clear relief, felt himself sag

along with her. They sighed simultaneously, looked at one another and smiled.

Dr Turner rose, stretched. 'It seems your girl has come through the worst of it.'

'I cannot thank you enough, Doctor. But she will recover fully? You are certain?'

'"Certain" is a tricky word, Mrs Albright. You say her health has suffered since you moved here? The air, you fear?'

'Yes, that is what I fear.'

'It is what I fear as well. She will recover this time, but as long as you live in the city there will be a risk to her health. The air in this neighbourhood, particularly, is not fit for children.'

Even though Clara apparently shared the doctor's opinion, Andrew knew this would be hard news for her to accept. In her mind she had no option but to remain where she was.

'Annabeth is having a good, healthy sleep now, but I will remain here for awhile, until later in the afternoon to be sure nothing changes.'

'It is kind of you to offer to stay, Doctor,' Clara said. 'But I have taken up enough of your time. Surely you have other patients?'

'None as sweet as this one. Besides, I left word where I might be found if anyone needs me.'

It would be hard to miss what was what was going

in Clara's mind now. She would be fretting over how she would pay the doctor's fee.

'My carriage is below, whenever you feel you can leave,' Andrew said.

'Let's see how the next few hours go.'

'Very well,' Clara agreed, her voice strained.

Unless Andrew missed his guess, she was calculating how many gowns she would need to sew in order to pay the doctor. It did not help that one which was to have been completed still lay untouched in the basket.

'May I have a word with you, Clara? In private?'

Andrew nodded towards the door. He would rather speak with her in the carriage, but at this hour Hinton might be still sleeping inside.

She walked ahead of him, out through the door and into the nearly dark corridor. It would be a while yet before the sun fully rose to give a bit of light to the space.

'I know you are worried about the doctor's fee, Clara,' he said. 'And it is only right that I should pay it.'

'It is wrong in every way I can think of. Annabeth is my child, not yours. Which makes little difference to the good doctor. He will expect to be paid before he leaves, so I suppose I must allow it. But I will reimburse you every penny, over time.'

'You can try to, of course, but I will not accept your money.'

'You must accept it. Really, Andrew, it is one thing for you to bring gifts to the children, but to pay my debt is not acceptable.'

'I am the one in debt to you. Remember, you would not be in this trouble had my brother not robbed you.'

Chapter Five

Clara sat down on the top stair with a great huff.

'The debt is on the soul of your black-hearted sibling. You are guilty of nothing.' The man really did bear a great deal of misplaced remorse, she thought. 'The more I get to know you, the more I know that you are nothing like Miles.'

'We had different fathers.'

Which explained everything and nothing.

'Tell me about yours.'

She wanted to know what had made this man who he was. It was important to know all she could about him, now that everything had changed for her once again. If Andrew would not give her back the money his brother took from her, which he was under no obligation to do anyway, she must consider what he had offered.

Marriage.

Marriage without love.

Since she had already experienced her once-in-a-lifetime love, she did not need another. Having that issue settled between them from the outset would be wise.

If this was, indeed, the outset.

Even though she feared this marriage might be inevitable in the end, she was still slow to accept the necessity. There was so much more to be considered in marriage than the state of their romance. A romance which did not exist.

In particular, she did not wish to give over her finances to a man…leave herself vulnerable to fate again.

'I have told you my father was a minister,' he said, with a smile that told her he was looking back, seeing the man in his mind. 'The best man I ever knew. When I was young, all I wanted was to be like Father. My mother was desperately in love with him. The grief of losing him nearly took her from me. My mother feels things quite intensely. Back then she swore she would never love again.'

'Yes, I understand your mother's feelings. I have also experienced my one true love. I have no need of another.'

By saying so was she setting a boundary for marriage? Perhaps inching closer to accepting his proposal?

'I would not ask you to love me.' He looked at her with a slight frown creasing his brow. 'In fact, I would rather you did not. But I do feel we might be friends. I believe that perhaps we already are.'

'Marrying out of obligation is not an easy thing for me, Andrew. I do not think it can be for you either.'

'I think a marriage of friendship would be a fine state to be in.'

'Perhaps you have ever been in love, then.'

He arched one brow, shook his head. 'I learned a great deal about the cost of love from my mother. After my father died she was severely distraught. It was a scoundrel who brought her out of it in the end. He was too charming by half, and broke as a mouse— even though he lived as if he were not. My stepfather was a long way into running through Mother's fortune when he died. That's when I took over managing our finances…all the while trying to lift her from deep depression. I swear, Clara, losing that faithless spendthrift was harder on her than losing my father. I think it is why she is so blinded when it comes to Miles. No matter what mischief he got into growing up, she doted on him, saying he was so like his father.'

'Did you try to make up for his misdeeds even as a boy?'

'Not on purpose. Over time I just fell into a pattern of trying to protect my mother from the man my brother really was.'

'You are a good son, Andrew. But your mother never knew what you were doing?'

'It wasn't so hard. Mother sees what she wishes to see with Miles, the same as she did with his father.'

'I hope she sees you too, and your own father in you. I think perhaps you are a good reflection of him.'

'Do you like me, Clara? It seems you do.'

She knew what he meant in asking…what he was leading up to. He was not seeking compliments. He was seeking a wife.

A draught from the gap under the door at the foot of the stairs whistled up the stairway. It always made it harder to keep her apartment warm. Just because it was nearly spring did not mean the weather was mild. Unfortunately, there was not much coal left in the bin. Not that she was overly worried. Andrew was here, and he would replace it if they ran out.

She knew she was becoming increasingly dependent upon this man. The question being, was she relieved by that or distressed?

One thing was clear. Being warm was better than being cold—especially when a sick child was involved.

'You have kept my family fed, brought them gifts,

rescued my son and now my daughter. Of course I like you.'

'Would you like me more if I had an estate in the country?'

'I would not.' She already knew him to be a decent man. His worldly goods did not change who he was at heart. But at the same time… 'Do you have one?'

'I do. It isn't terribly far from London by train. It's a beautiful place, Clara. The air is clean, and so fresh you could sit on the veranda and breathe it in all day, just for the pure pleasure of it.'

'You are a fortunate man, Andrew.'

'Indeed I am. But did you notice that I said *you* could sit on the veranda—not that I could sit on it?'

Oh, she had noticed. And in that instant, her heart had gone wandering, landing her smack down on that veranda, breathing deeply and gazing out at rolling green vistas.

'The reason I have mentioned the estate is not to influence you with my wealth. It's because Dr Turner has told us that Annabeth needs to live somewhere with healthy air.'

Clara was far too aware of the fact. However, there were other matters to be considered before she consented to entrusting her life, and the lives of her family, to this man.

Were the advantages of marrying Andrew worth the risks? That was what she must consider.

There was no denying they would be safe with Andrew, well fed and comfortable. However, she was not foolish enough to believe it could not end suddenly...tragically.

Then where would they be? Unless she had a hand in managing the family finances, she might easily become ruined again.

'Think about it...' Andrew went on. 'Annabeth would grow up in a healthy place. George would not run off to work in a factory. Lilly would have all the gowns she needed. Many of my neighbours are peers so she would have her choice of beaus.'

'Do not think I have not considered all those things.'

'Why, then, do you hesitate?'

She was quiet for a moment, weighing everything in her mind...again.

'So, you will solve all our problems and get exactly what in return? Other than appeasing misplaced guilt for your brother's crime, I cannot see the benefit to you.' She shivered in the cold draught again.

'Not so misplaced, Clara. Perhaps I coddled him for my mother's sake when it was a strict hand he needed.'

'Perhaps it was your stepfather's job to do that. How old was Miles when he died?'

'Ten years old. Same as I was when my father died.'

'Ah, well, then. Your father formed who you were and his father formed who he was. Honestly, Andrew, I doubt there was anything you could have done to change him.'

'Whether I could have or could not have is irrelevant. Miles is my blood and he has wronged you.'

'You do not need to right that wrong by becoming responsible for me and my family for the rest of your life. As we have discussed before, you can simply repay the money.'

'Unscrupulous men might try and take it from you.'

'Marriage cannot prevent that from happening.'

They were silent for a moment, their opposing views putting them at an impasse.

'There is something I will gain by our marriage. And it has nothing to do with my brother,' he said at last. 'Everything to do with my mother, though.'

'You need help in caring for your mother?'

Somehow this made her feel better about marrying him. There would be something she could give back to him. The idea of him giving all and she giving nothing was not acceptable.

He took her hand, held it. She did not mind. His fingers were long, warm, and swallowed hers up. They were discussing marriage, so it seemed that there should be some sort of affection displayed between them. Given that the affection was not love, she did not draw back from his touch.

'She cannot remain in London. If you agree to our marriage we will all live in the country. The move is necessary for her as well as for Annabeth. I'm afraid that if my mother hears about what Miles did she will be broken once again. At her age I wonder if she would recover. If we remain here it will not be long before she learns the truth. But what I hope is that you, your sister and the children will take up so much room in her heart she will not miss Miles so much.'

'What a hard situation for you, Andrew. But will keeping the news from her work? Even in the country? People will still talk.'

'The staff will not say anything, and perhaps if we limit visitors…'

We? As in Andrew and Clara? Hmm… Until this moment she had given no thought to how nice their names sounded together. Not that it was either here or there when it came to deciding whether to wed the man or not.

'She believes Miles has gone on a long holiday. So the one thing I would ask of you, if you agree to marry me, is that you do not speak of my brother's crime. I know it is not fair to ask it of you, but I must.'

'I fear that one day you will resent me, Andrew. You think that you do not require love in a marriage.

But how can you know that? Have you really never been in love?'

'Once. That is how I know I do not require it.'

Good, then. Neither did she. Not this time. What she needed was what he offered. Security for her family.

He squeezed her hand. With the growing light in the corridor, she saw how sincere his gaze upon her was.

Very well, then. The time had come to make a decision—if there had ever been one to make.

In the space of a held breath she weighed everything one more time. The reasons for marrying Andrew and the reasons for not.

When it came down to it…her children's needs mattered most. Every reason he presented in favour of this marriage was correct. George would attend a proper school. Lilly would meet a proper beau. Most of all, Annabeth would breathe easily.

Giving over financial control to her husband was not what she wished, what she felt comfortable with, but so be it.

Needs were what needs were.

'Your mother will hear nothing of her son's treachery from me. I promise you, that, Andrew.'

She felt it when his breath hitched, when his fingers clenched around her hand.

'Mrs Albright, are you saying you will marry me?

He lifted her hand to his lips, kissed her fingers. 'Dare I hope you will become Mrs Benton?'

'Yes, Andrew. Mrs Benton I will be. There is only one thing I require.'

It was not much. And it amounted to nothing more than the suggestion of financial independence.

'I understand that everything I have is legally yours. But what I wish is for you to agree, between us, is that whatever money I bring into our marriage will remain mine to control.'

As pitiful an amount as it was.

'Agreed. I promise you will not be sorry. I will be a responsible husband.'

She knew women who'd had much less going into a marriage.

'So, then, we are going into this with an understanding between us.'

'Indeed. We will require nothing more from one another than friendship and loyalty.' His smile was bright, pleased. 'We are beginning our lives together quite sensibly, don't you agree?'

She nodded. 'Sensibly, yes. Thoughtfully and level-headed.'

With that, he placed a quick, warm kiss on her chilled lips.

She could do without romantic love.

Except that when he'd kissed her she'd felt her heart stretch its rusty wings, if only for an instant.

The scent of his skin, the feel of his breath in the second before he'd kissed her, made her feel something akin to desire.

A rekindled echo of the past, and no more.

'Seemed the proper thing to do upon becoming engaged,' he said, with a smile even warmer than his lips had been. 'I hope you don't mind?'

She shook her head, and blinked at the long-forgotten tickle along her nerves. 'I don't mind.'

'Let's go back inside and share our news.' He helped her up from the cold wooden stair. 'We will wed right away and then go to my estate. I will not have you living here an hour longer than you must.'

Perhaps this marriage would work out for the best. And in time she might have the one thing she had despaired of having.

Another child.

She and Andrew did not need to be in love to accomplish that end. They had kissed without being in love, so perhaps…

The next morning Clara, Lilly and the children got into Andrew's elegant carriage, leaving behind the life of scavenging on these mean streets and bouncing towards something more like the life they'd had two years ago.

'Look, Mother!' George exclaimed, pointing his finger excitedly. 'It's our old home.'

Assuming they would be passing it by, she had been preparing her heart for this moment. Her first thought had been to refuse to look at it. She was leaving her past behind. All of it. Good and bad. But in the moment she found it was difficult to put the good behind her as readily as the bad. She had thought she'd done it already, but the lump swelling in her throat told her perhaps she had not.

Clara had to look. How could she not?

Goodbye, Spencer...goodbye, home of my heart.

'Wait and see, Georgie,' Lilly said. 'The house we are going to is every bit as nice. I've seen it, so I know.'

'It's the country estate I want to see.'

George looked away from his old home. It was evident by the excitement in his expression that he was not giving the place an emotional farewell.

'Andrew says there is a stable full of horses which I can ride. And green hills to ride them over...and streams with fish.'

'He told me we will have affluent neighbours.' Lilly looked as excited as George did.

Annabeth was still too ill to join in the conversation. Clara had been promised that Dr Turner would be waiting for them when they arrived at Andrew's home. That was what she was grateful for.

'We talked about this last night, but it bears a reminder,' she said. 'We must be mindful not to say anything truthful about Miles. It is the one thing Andrew has asked of us. His mother is devoted to her younger son and would be crushed to discover what he really is.'

'I'll be too busy having adventures to give him a thought,' George declared.

'And you will not wish to let Andrew down. None of us will,' she said.

'It might be the hardest thing I have ever done, sister...' Lilly's wary expression showed her heart all too well.

'With an elderly woman's wellbeing at risk, we will not fail. From what Andrew says, his mother will be plunged into despair if the truth comes out. We shall be diligent in making sure that miserable reprobate does not claim another victim.'

'Yes,' Lilly agreed, sounding determined. 'And he is in prison, so it is not as if we will encounter him.'

Not soon, at least.

Before she could sink too deeply into thoughts of the awful future event, the carriage came to a halt.

'We are here,' Lilly announced.

Andrew stood at the front door. A short, round woman stood close to him. Obviously his mother. On his other side was Dr Turner.

Her groom-to-be had promised he would be a responsible husband, and the presence of the doctor was proof of it.

His mother's posture, the way she leaned ever so slightly towards him, spoke of her trust in him.

Although she did not know Andrew all that well—and perhaps she should, since she had agreed to share her life with him—she was certain he was a man to be relied upon.

'Well, then,' she said. 'Let's go and meet our future.'

The carriage door opened.

George leaped out with a whoop.

No sooner had Clara stepped out of the carriage than Andrew's mother clapped her hands, clearly delighted by the turn her life was taking.

At breakfast this morning Andrew had told her he was to be married, and that the lady came with two children and a sister. For the space of a blink, his mother had appeared stunned. She'd asked if he was certain, and when he had assured her he was, she had stood up and made one, slow spin while clapping her hands.

It was never enough for Mother simply to smile her pleasure. She expressed it with her whole body.

'I am to have a family!'

He'd arched a brow at her, puzzled. 'I was not aware you did not have one already.'

'You know what I mean. Now I will have a complete family, with children and other females. Thank you, Andrew. You and Miles are such dear sons.'

Hinton reached into the carriage. He picked up Annabeth and carried her to the door.

His mother's cheeks turned pink with pleasure. 'Oh, Andrew! I adore them already. You have done quite well,' she whispered. 'I do hope they take to me.'

'Everyone takes to you,' he whispered back. 'The same way you take to everyone.'

'But naturally! There is so much to love in people.'

With that, she bustled down the steps.

Before a proper introduction could be made she took each of the people coming up the path by the shoulders, gave them a great smile, then enveloped them in a hug.

'I have been praying you would come for so long.'

If the comment surprised anyone they did not say so.

'Mother has been hoping I would marry for a long time,' he clarified.

'What a great pleasure it is to meet you, Mrs Benton,' Clara said, giving his mother a second hug…a longer one.

If a man was meant to fall in love, a sight such as this one would be the spark, he thought. Not that when he'd impulsively kissed her the other day on the stairs it hadn't sizzled.

It seemed he would need to walk a fine line between liking his wife and falling in love with her. He must be careful not to lose his balance.

'If only my Miles could be here,' Mother said. 'He would adore you all.'

Clara bit her lip. Lilly glanced at the sky, appearing to study a passing cloud.

'He is away, isn't he?' Clara asked.

Andrew's heart went to his throat, swelled until he thought he would choke. *Please, Clara, please keep the secret.*

'On business, Andrew says? I look forward to seeing him again.'

That could mean anything. But to give him what for was what she must be thinking.

'You have met my darling boy?'

'Oh, indeed. He and my first husband were acquainted, so we did meet upon occasion.'

'How wonderful, my dear. And just when I thought I could be no happier.'

His mother's smile was innocent, reflecting nothing but joy.

'I only hope Miles is not gone for terribly long. It is hard to know with that charming lad of mine. He comes and goes.'

'I shall be pleased to meet Uncle Miles,' George said, with a sidelong glance at Clara.

Mother pressed George's cheeks between her soft, lined hands, shaping his lips into a funny-looking pucker. 'What a dear boy you are. I will thank God for you in my prayers tonight.'

True to form, his mother had opened her heart to them. From all he could see, Clara and her family were fitting right in.

By the time Hinton was halfway up the path with Annabeth, Dr Turner had rushed to meet them.

Mother walked beside Annabeth, going up the steps and into the house. All the way she cooed and fussed over her new little granddaughter.

Clara fell into step beside Andrew, slipping her hand into the crook of his arm. It felt like the most natural touch in the world. Friendly...acceptable in every way.

'Your mother might be the most welcoming person I have ever met.'

He gave her hand a pat. 'Thank you...about Miles, I mean.'

'I thought I would choke on my words, if you want to know the truth. But of course I would not hurt your mother for the world. And not only for your sake, Andrew. Now that I have met her, I understand. I will be very careful.'

'I wish for us to marry immediately. I have made arrangements to go to Gretna Green.'

'Elope, do you mean?'

'I do. I mean that exactly. The sooner we remove to the countryside, the better.'

'It's a bold one you are, Andrew Benton. Making such plans…' She held him to the spot with that way she had of staring down her nose at him, even though he was the taller one. 'But I will not elope with you.'

Even with the stern look she was giving him, he saw moisture brighten her eyes.

Wasn't he a dunce of the first order?

Clara had been in love the first time she'd married. Running away with her groom had been pure romance. He ought to have realised going back to Gretna Green would cause her grief.

'Of, course…you will want the time to have a proper gown made,' he said.

Perhaps she would, but his intention in saying so was to draw her back from the past. To the here and now, where love would never again break her heart.

'I should have thought. How long will you need, my

dear? I will have my mother's seamstress come this afternoon, if you wish.'

'I will not move into your home and then take my good time before wedding you. Rest assured I am as eager to move to the estate as you are. But I will not elope again.'

'Forgive me, Clara. It was thoughtless of me to suggest it. I know you loved Spencer. We will not do anything to tarnish the memoires you have of him.'

'But I do need time to find a proper gown. When I wed the first time, I wore the dress I ran away in. You will have a bride who looks like one. But do not call for a seamstress. I will sew it myself.'

'You no longer need to. I can well afford to have your gowns made.'

She stopped walking when they were halfway across the grand hall. The others went on, deeper into the house.

'I know you can. It is only that I cannot simply go back to being the woman I used to be…' She glanced about as if making certain they were alone. Then she whispered, 'Before Miles.'

'I promise to make it up to you ten times over.'

'What must I do to convince you it is not your place to try? It cannot be done, at any rate.'

'I suppose it is forgiveness I am seeking.'

Funny how it had only now occurred to him that that was what he was after.

She reached up, touched his cheek with the backs of her fingers. 'Can you tell me one instance which you must be forgiven for?'

'My brother—'

She shook her head, frowned. Red ringlets framed her face in the sweetest way, offsetting the frown. 'You cannot name one,' she said. 'And now the matter is put to rest.'

'Thank you for saying so…and for protecting my mother. Miles does not deserve it. If it weren't for her I would—'

'No more talk of him. We will deal with him as the need arises. For now, we will think about getting married.'

In a proper ceremony. One in which she was consulted about the details. It was not just his own life he was making decisions for any more, after all.

'When would be a good time for our wedding to take place?' he asked. 'Will you wish for flowers and music? I would like to have them if they can be had at short notice.'

'Flowers and music would be lovely, Andrew. I had neither of those the first time. I believe I would enjoy them.'

Clara nodded, indicating the matter was settled.

She took a few steps after the rest of the family, then paused, cast a glace over her shoulder.

'It will not take me long to sew my gown. By the time you make the arrangements I will be ready. And now I will beg your mother for a tour of this beautiful home.'

Plain brown homespun swayed as she walked away. Satin and lace would not swish over her hips in a more intriguing manner.

Andrew struggled to keep his mouth from sagging, his gaze from lingering where it was not wise.

It was all he could do to catch his breath and remind himself that this was to be a friendly union, not a passionate one.

Chapter Six

The course of one's life, Andrew observed rather poetically, could change on the turn of a breeze.

And if one could not wax poetic on one's wedding day, he could not imagine when one could.

Poetic, he assured himself, was not the same thing as romantic.

Only three weeks after she'd arrived in Mayfair, Clara Albright had become Clara Benton.

His to have and to hold, to protect and to cherish.

His vows that morning had not been insincere, since one could cherish a wife without being in love with her.

The wedding had been simple, the vows direct, yet touching. Flowers and music had added quite a bit to make the occasion special for a couple who were committing themselves to one another without the complication of romance.

After a wedding breakfast to celebrate the creation

of a new family, they had boarded two coaches—one for Mother and the children and the other for him and his bride. While train travel would have been the quickest way to get to the village near the estate, the privacy of the coach felt more appropriate for the day.

Looking at Clara now, Andrew could only wonder how this resplendent woman could be the same lady who had accepted his proposal while sitting on a creaky stair, shivering in a dress that had been too thin to keep her warm.

Cinderella risen from the ashes. That is what she reminded him of. But he had known her before. In those days he had been impressed with her charm and beauty.

Clara had gone from exquisite, to pragmatic, and now to a fascinating combination of the two. If he had not been a man who feared loss he might not have been able to resist her. Luckily, he had a rather strong will.

'I'm glad you decided to wear your wedding gown for our ride to the country. It is lovely.'

'Indeed, one of my best. I'll not be meeting your staff in rags.'

She skimmed her fingers over the line of pearls dotting the bodice from the collar to the sash at her waist. Her soft smile nearly knocked him off the bench, if such a thing were even possible.

'It was a lovely wedding, Andrew. Thank you for all you did to make it so.'

The wedding had been as close to romantic as he could get without crossing the line. He'd wanted to please his wife without wandering into forbidden territory. She did not wish for that sort of marriage any more than he did. Having loved and lost, she was wise enough to avoid that sort of grief a second time.

And because they were in agreement on the issue, it boded very well for a deep friendship between them.

Just because he would not be head-over-coattails in love with his wife, it did not mean Clara Benton would lack for love.

His mother adored her new daughter, and all who came with her, and she did it, as always, without reserve.

They had left the city behind now, and the land had become greener, the air fresher. He knew his mother, along with Lilly and the children, would be pleased. Anyone would prefer the country to the city.

'I am anxious to see the estate, Andrew,' Clara said. 'Is it terribly isolated? I have only lived in London. My father did not like the country so we only had our home in London. But it was really all we could afford anyway. I hardly know what to expect at the estate.'

'There will not be as much noise, and not a lot of people, either. No fish vendors or factories.'

'I will not miss those things. But I cannot say for certain that I will enjoy the lack of society.'

'There will be society of sorts, but it will not be pressing upon us every moment.'

He watched her gazing out of the window and wondered exactly what she was thinking. She had wed him of necessity...was moving to a place which was foreign to her because it was best for everyone else. What did she think of the pastures going by the window? Did she see a haven and a refuge or a place of lonely isolation?

'I will do my best to make you happy there,' he said.

'Oh, I shall do well enough as long as I do not encounter a bull wandering the estate grounds...that *is* a bull out there, isn't it?' She pointed her finger at a large one, grazing on a hill in the distance. 'I am not at all familiar with livestock, Andrew.'

'You are more likely to encounter a sheep. And lambs are charming creatures, as you will see.'

'Well, I imagine the children will find them so.' She returned her attention to looking out of the window. 'It is pretty...if uncivilised.'

Hopefully once she saw her new home and met the staff she would not think his estate uncivilised. The village near his estate was a picture of charm and civility. Elmbrook even had a train station.

'If you long for London we can be there in little more than an hour by train.'

'Do not think I am ungrateful for all you have done for us, Andrew. This is just all so different from what I am used to. It's so big and wide open.'

She glanced away from the window, reached for his hand and squeezed it, her smile as soft and inviting as the afternoon sunshine streaking the window.

'I have every intention of being happy here.'

All well and good, but good intentions were only that. A person could not *decide* to be happy. He was not bringing her here to be miserable. He meant it to be for the good of the children and for his mother.

'Clara, tell me…what I can do to make sure you are?'

'Oh, that will be easy enough.' She cocked her head, gave him another sweet smile. 'I need to feel secure. If I have that, being happy will fall into place.'

'Secure? As my wife you will always be safe. I'll not let anything happen to you or the children.'

'I believe that is your intention. But you need to know that Spencer told me the same thing on the day we wed, and I believed him. They were lovely words, and I put my faith in them. I do not need to tell you what happened… You are a married man because of it.'

'Just because something happened once, it does not mean it will happen again.'

'Nor does it guarantee it will not. And you did ask what you could do.'

All of a sudden he wished he hadn't. The arch of her brows and the determined set of her mouth warned him that it was likely to be something he would need to refuse.

Then, like mist dissolving in sunshine, her expression changed, became soft and engaging. He was certain she had changed tactics deliberately, and was now trying to charm him into getting what she wanted.

His wife was lovely when she was charming…even if it was not quite genuine.

'I would like to have a hand in managing your finances.'

If only she had asked for a world tour! It only now occurred to him that he had not planned a honeymoon. But a honeymoon indicated a certain sort of behaviour which was not in the best interests of their marriage.

What she asked was impossible, of course. Managing the financial matters of the estate and the business was not at all the same thing as being in charge of the small amount of money she'd had before they married.

'What would I do with my accountant? It would not be right to put him out of employment. Joseph has a large family to support.'

'Please tell me you do not put all your faith in someone else to look after your money!'

'I am aware of where every penny is spent. You need not fear.'

'So long as you are walking this earth, I will not.'

This conversation was taking a grim turn. He hoped to be walking the earth for a very long time—especially now that he was a husband and father.

'Perhaps Cook will not mind if you take an interest in the kitchen accounts.'

Please let this satisfy her, he thought. He truly did want to her to be happy as his wife.

'I shall speak with her about it.'

From a quarter of a mile away Clara spotted the manor house coming into view. It looked like a jewel nestled into a hilltop. A couple of dozen windows caught the last rays of sunshine, as if giving the day a wink of goodbye.

'Do you like it?' Andrew asked.

It was good to hear him speak. They hadn't had much to say to one another since their discussion about her having a hand in his finances.

Clearly he was at a loss as to how to answer her perfectly reasonable request.

She hadn't had much to say to him, either. Because

how was she to argue putting a family man out of his position?

And now, seeing the size of her new home, and all the acres of land they had crossed simply to arrive at the front door, she did have to admit that managing her own meagre finances did not qualify her for this. With the town house, the estate and Andrew's business, it would take two accountants to keep it all going.

Which did not in any way mean she was giving up on what she wanted. Having knowledge of Andrew's finances was crucial to the future of everyone she loved. However, biding her time made a great deal of sense. Until she knew more about her new home and what went into its care and keeping, learning about the finances that kept it afloat would be impossible.

If she tried to look at them too soon, she would appear incompetent.

But between this moment and the one she hoped would soon present itself, she would learn all she could.

'Oh, Andrew, your home is breathtaking.'

'I hope you are not intimidated by its size. Inside, it's as cosy as a nest.'

A nest she hoped her children would not get lost in. Spencer's town house in London had been spacious, but it did not compare to this.

However, what it looked besides big was safe. The

chances of a thief or a lady of the night wandering past the window were exceptionally unlikely.

As long as she encountered a lamb rather than a bull, she was likely to be quite secure. In fact, there was every chance she would venture out after dinner just to experience the unique sensation.

The carriage slowed, then stopped in front the house. It did not appear as large as it had from a distance. Sunlight had faded from the windows with the creeping dusk, but now lamplight shone warmly out of them in welcome.

No sooner had the carriage carrying her mother-in-law and the children stopped behind them than the servants hustled out through the front door and lined up in greeting.

'It's cold, Andrew. Tell them they need not do this.'

He took her hand, pressed it into the crook of his arm. 'I could not convince them to go inside even if I pleaded. You can't imagine their curiosity over you. I believe they gave up hope of having a mistress in this home a long time ago.'

This sort of social interaction had been natural to her at one time, but she was having a little difficulty reviving her familiarity with it. At one time she had been the lady of an elegant home, with important visitors to entertain. Nonetheless, now she was stumbling over greeting staff. It must be because she had so recently been below their rank.

But even if in this moment she did not feel like the mistress of this home, she knew what to do to look as if she did. Smile. Look into each person's eyes. Repeat their name and make them feel appreciated.

Which they were. She would be grateful for every service performed for her in a way she would not have been before the 'fall'.

'Welcome home, Mrs Benton.'

The greeting came from Andrew.

Glancing up, she saw him grinning at her, his expression warmer than the glow in the windows.

She crooked her finger at him, as if she wished to whisper in his ear. When he bent his head, she placed a kiss on his cheek.

'Home sweet home,' she said. 'I can hardly wait to get inside.'

All at once she was wrapped up in a hug—and not from Andrew. This hug was soft, plush, and from her mother-in-law.

'Young love is the sweetest thing in the world,' she murmured.

Clara smiled. The last thing she was going to do was disappoint the lady by pointing out the facts. Those being that she and her son were not all that young and they were certainly not in love. More, that the only reason they had wed was because of what her darling Miles had done to her.

'Indeed, it is,' she answered.

Mother took George by the hand and walked through a tall doorway, chatting happily.

'I'm sorry for that, Clara. My mother is—'

'She is correct, Andrew. It is the sweetest thing in the world to be in love. I remember.'

'Also the hardest thing to lose.'

'Agreed,' she mumbled, as he led her into her new home for the first time.

Until arriving at his estate, Clara had not fully understood how wealthy her new husband was. Apparently there was a great deal of money to be made in selling fabric. Much more than there was in sewing it.

After tucking George into his big, soft bed in his very own chamber, and then doing the same for Annabeth, Clara went to her own chamber and sank wearily into the great soft chair in front of the fire, which someone had already lit.

What a long, eventful day it had been. She had become a married woman again. After that she'd moved her family to a new home. And all between sunrise and sunset.

She listened for a moment, appreciating the peaceful quiet beyond her first-floor window.

Dinner had been amazing. The kitchen staff had brought out course after course of delicious food. Andrew's London cook was talented, but the country cook… Well, Clara might lie awake wondering what would be for breakfast.

During her two years as a pauper she had become unaccustomed to fine living. One thing was for certain: she would never take a meal for granted. Nor would she completely regret her struggle during those years. She was a stronger woman for them, and certainly more appreciative of where she was now, and for every single little thing a servant did for her.

Andrew's chamber was beside hers. There was a door connecting the two rooms which was locked and would remain so.

She could hear him moving about, speaking with someone. His valet, she supposed.

Clara had Della Grey to see to her needs. The young maid had turned down the covers of her bed, then spread her nightclothes across the mattress.

The plush and inviting mattress.

The mattress she would not be sharing with her sister and her daughter.

Not her husband either.

Only moments ago she had dismissed Della. Surely the girl had a better way of spending her evening than helping Clara into her nightgown…a task which

Clara was able to do for herself. Perhaps one day she would get used to being fussed over again, but it was not tonight.

Rising from her chair, she went to the bed, sat upon it with a thump. The mattress cradled her derriere, plush, lump-free and inviting. It even had a light and lovely scent. Lavender, she guessed.

She undressed, put on her sleeping gown and her robe. They were worn, having been with her through all her life's changes.

Apparently there was a seamstress coming tomorrow, to measure everyone for new clothes. That would be interesting. She was well able to design and sew her own clothes. However, her new station made it more appropriate to employ others. Now that she was once again a lady of funds, it was her duty to spread those funds.

Passing the window, she paused to look down at the acres of grass and trees illuminated by a bright full moon. Earlier, she'd thought about going outside. Having had no experience of living in the country, she'd wondered what it would be like…listening to the sounds of the night, comparing them to the two areas of London she had lived in.

Very well. This was her home now, and she was anxious to get to know it. And what a perfect time to explore, since her attention would not be distracted by little ones needing her attention.

Quietly, she left her chamber, tiptoed down the stairs and then went out through a set of doors at the back of the house leading to a veranda.

The first thing she noticed while standing at the top of the veranda steps was the solitude.

It was rare not to be in the presence of another person. Everywhere in London one was within speaking distance of someone else. In her home there had been no privacy whatsoever.

Standing still, she listened to the sounds of a country night.

At first all she heard was nothing. But then, after closing her eyes, breathing as slowly and as quietly as possible, she heard the grass. It made whispery sounds when a breeze blew over it.

Her robe ruffled about her, flapping happily—or that was how she interpreted it at any rate.

She opened her arms to feel fresh air passing around her, so cool and invigorating. Breathing deeply, she thought the difference between the country and the city was clear.

Opening her eyes, she saw more stars than could be counted. An eternity of them.

Standing there, simply breathing, she felt as if her lungs were cleansed. This was why Dr Turner had said

Annabeth must live in the country. And tomorrow she would bring her child outside to continue her healing.

Looking across the long, wide swath of grass, she spotted a copse of trees on the rise of a hill. Next to the trees was a large stable, and a big paddock divided into three sections.

What a wonderful thing it was to look out at land shimmering in the moonlight without seeing a vagrant sneaking about.

Seeing only lush grass which looked as soft as a thousand yards of velvet.

It would feel wonderful on bare feet. And as luck would have it, her feet were bare.

Hurrying down the steps, she felt lighter than she had in…oh…far too long to recall. Some sort of weight had been lifted from her.

She walked through the grass, enjoying the tickle between her toes, wondering what that missing weight had been.

And if the grass felt this good on her feet, how much better would it feel if she were lying down in it?

There was only one way to know, so she sat down… ran her fingers over the blades. The scent of green wafted up, and she lay down and spread her arms wide.

It was cold, but never mind that. She wanted to look at the stars.

Looking into the dark above, which was not really dark with all the diamond-like twinkling, she felt everything in her slow down.

She realised what the missing weight had been.

Fear.

Her family was safe here. She closed her eyes, heard a sheep bleating and another answering.

'Thank you, Andrew,' she said aloud.

A blanket floated down over her.

'You are welcome. I am not sure what for, though.'

Why was she lying in the grass, shivering and saying thank you to him?

Especially since she had spoken when she hadn't even been aware of him standing there.

She smiled, as if she were not startled to see him.

'Have you come out to watch the stars with me?'

She lifted the corner of the blanket.

It was his wedding night, so why should he not at least lie beside his wife and gaze at the heavens.

A few reasons presented themselves. It was cold, it could be mistaken for being romantic...and she was not dressed.

He shrugged, ignored the reasons, and sat down beside her.

The last point hardly mattered, since the lady was his wife. And the cold would be less biting with two people under the blanket. As for being romantic...their time together might just as well be taken as friendly.

He would make sure that was what it was.

'If you lie down you can see the stars without hurting your neck,' she pointed out.

Good sense was good sense, so he lay down, folding his arms behind his head to form a pillow.

'What were you thanking me for?' he asked.

'For marrying me and bringing my family here, where Annabeth can breathe. I cannot say what a relief it is that there are no factories for Georgie to run off to. And you must know that Lilly is beside herself at being measured for new gowns tomorrow. I was thanking you for all those things.'

A star shot across the sky, bright and streaking from horizon to horizon. They both pointed their fingers at it at the same time.

'And I am thanking you for not accepting my refusals of your proposals.'

Under the blanket, warmth passed between them. Probably more from him to her, since he had been heated before he'd even came down.

He'd been watching through the window when she'd come outside. That was how he'd known to bring a blanket. When she had lifted her arms and the breeze had fluttered her gown about her figure the worn garment had showed it to be a very fine one. Full in places he appreciated, and trim in others.

His wife was an appealing woman.

It might take some effort to keep in mind that they were, and must remain, friends.

'I thank you too, Clara.'

'Do you?' she asked, with her gaze still set on the stars. 'Why? You are the one to have given so much.'

'I've been meaning to speak of it all evening, but the opportunity never came. It's for not revealing what Miles really is. Especially when you have every right to speak bitterly about him.'

'Perhaps I do. But what I do not have the right to do is break your mother's heart. Truly, Andrew, I would never speak ill of any woman's child. As a mother myself, I know how it would cut to the heart.'

'You are a kind woman. Your children are proof. I can't believe how they're keeping the secret so well.'

'They haven't had a grandmother before and are over the moon.' She sighed.

The space under the blanket was warming nicely.

'This is lovely, Andrew. We should make a habit of it.'

'I used to do this when I was a boy. It was after my father died. Never had any company then, though. I used to hope he would somehow make himself known to me among the stars.'

'I can understand that. It's as if you can see all the way to eternity.' She turned her face towards him. 'Did it help? Did he make himself known?'

'Hard to tell. One time I asked that if he could see me would he make a star shoot across the sky. One did, right after I asked, so I took it as my father. I've seen hundreds of them since, so perhaps it wasn't him at all.'

'We shall say it was.' She shifted onto her side, lifting up on her elbow to look down at him. 'Perhaps shooting stars are loved ones making a merry show of eternity?'

Her hair was loose, and a curly strand hung over her shoulder.

'Your hair is very pretty, Clara. Would you take it amiss if I touched it?'

She smiled, held the strand between her fingers, then tickled his nose with it. He drew it from between her fingers, let it glide across his palm. Better than silk. He was well-acquainted with silk so he knew.

'I did not realise you were so playful, Clara.'

'I used to be…once upon a time.'

She had sparkled. He remembered quite clearly.

'It seems to be coming back to you.'

'It must be all that beauty up there. It's difficult to be sober-minded with heavenly glitter in your eyes.'

'Are you ready to go back inside? It is growing cold.'

'Not yet. You go, if you wish. I think I shall watch for Spencer to give me a wink.'

'If you can bear the cold, so can I. It has been for ever since I've lain here simply to look up.'

Before he had finished speaking, a huge star shot overhead, brighter than any he had seen before.

'Was that him, do you think?' he asked.

She turned her face to him with a smile. 'Spencer was a bold one too, so perhaps it was. We shall say so, at any rate.'

'I'm glad your husband came to say hello.'

'My *late* husband. My husband is lying beside me in the grass.'

Nothing would be nicer in that moment than kissing her, he thought. He could not help but wonder what she would do if he tried.

Quite suddenly it was too hot under the blanket.

'It is getting chilly, Clara. We must go inside. I will not have you becoming unwell.'

Getting to his feet, he plucked up the blanket, reached a hand down and helped his bride to stand. It was not possible that starlight lingered in her hair, shone from her eyes, but it seemed like it to him.

He set the blanket around her shoulders, tucked it under her chin, because it truly was cold now.

Also because her sleeping gown was threadbare.

How much temptation could friendship take before it changed into something else? Something hot and risky?

That was one thing he was not willing to discover.

Chapter Seven

Three weeks after her illness, Annabeth was recovered enough to go outdoors, to run, play and laugh.

While Lilly bade goodbye to the gentleman who had come to call, chaperoned by both her own maid and Clara's, the rest of the new family took a walk to the barn

'I want to see the lambs, Papa!' said Annabeth.

Clara's heart squeezed. Her step faltered.

Her child had had a father. She'd used to call him Papa in her baby voice. But, having been so young when he died, Annabeth no longer remembered him, and it twisted her heart to hear Spencer's child call another man Papa.

But after all Andrew had done for Annabeth he deserved to bear the title. No father could have served her better when she had been sick almost to death.

Oh, but Spencer had adored it when she'd called

him that…how could Clara help but be jealous for him?

It had been two years since she'd put her grief away, but every once in a while it doubled back on her. Cut her when she least expected it.

Andrew had scooped Annabeth up, was twirling about with her in his arms. Annabeth giggled. It had been far too long since she had heard her daughter do that.

If she felt anything on Spencer's behalf, it ought to be gratitude.

'And I bet there is a lamb who cannot wait to make your acquaintance,' Andrew said, then set Annabeth down.

George was racing uphill towards the barn.

Annabeth and Andrew ran after him.

Clara stood where she was, watching them, a small lump swelling in her chest.

This was not how she had expected her family to be…*where* she'd expected them to be. When she'd used to imagine the future it had always been Spencer playing with his children in their London garden.

Her late husband might or might not be pleased that Andrew had stepped in for him, but she was. And she was the one who was living this life. For all she knew, Spencer's spirit was galloping up the hill along with Andrew and the children.

Regardless of whether it was or not, she was going to join them. And with her heart swelling in a curious combination of joy and regret, she dashed after them.

She had a new life now. There would be times when past memories intruded—it was natural for that to happen. But Andrew was waiting for her at the top of the hill.

Running up the slope, she knew that, in time, the memories she was making now would be as precious as the old ones.

Winded, she neared the rise. Andrew held out his hand to her.

Annabeth and George had already gone into the barn. She heard their voices, sounding excited. A man was speaking to them.

'That's Bosing, my farmer. He will be in a special sort of heaven, showing the lambs off to the children. I think he loves the small creatures as much as the ewes do.'

Because of the bright light outside, the interior of the barn seemed dim while her eyes adjusted to the change.

Andrew led her to a bench near the lambs' pen, her hand nicely cradled in his. He sat beside her, gave her fingers a squeeze before releasing them.

After a moment she was able to see more clearly. Annabeth sat on a chair in the pen and Bosing was lifting a lamb onto her lap. George sat on the floor, apparently not concerned about what might get smeared on his trousers.

Well, it was a happy sight, even so. At their London home the only animals the children had encountered were dead fish and the occasional stray cat.

She turned to Andrew, but her smile sagged when she saw his expression.

'What is it, Andrew?'

He looked far too serious to be in the presence of tiny frolicking sheep. Surely the sweet bleating was enough to make any person's heart happy.

George's clearly was. He seemed nearly beside himself with mirth, now having three lambs at one time on his lap.

This was a far better life for a child than working in a factory. There were too many who did. Thanks to Andrew, Georgie would not be among them.

'Is something troubling you?' she asked.

'Annabeth called me Papa.'

He shook his head, a pair of frown lines cutting his brow. She'd never seen a frown that looked handsome before, but there it was—plain to see.

'You do not wish to be called Papa?' For all that hearing it had taken her aback a moment ago, she was disappointed that he did not wish for Annabeth to call him that.

'I do! Very much. But I do not want to overstep. Shall I speak with her about it?'

'Andrew Benton! If anyone deserves to be called Papa it is you.'

In that moment she wanted to kiss him, to impress upon him how very right it was for Annabeth to call him that. But then, that might not be all the reason. She would make her point without a kiss. Otherwise she would be the one overstepping.

So she kept her lips to herself. Except to use them to say, 'I would be pleased—no…grateful for you to call my children son and daughter. No one has done more for them than you have. Not even their father.'

'Surely not?'

'I do not mean that quite as it sounded. He did love and care for them, and it was his greatest pleasure. But it was also his duty. Andrew, it was not your duty to do what you did, and yet you did not hesitate to help them.'

'I believe it *was* my duty. After—'

She touched one finger to his lips, shook her head.

'Do not tell me you did it to make up for your brother. I know better. I know who you are.'

For a long moment he simply looked at her without speaking—which might have had to do with her finger keeping him from doing so.

He had nice lips. The top one was thin, but the bottom one was full, plush...

What was she doing? She snatched her finger back.

'Do you think George will call me Papa?' he asked.

'He remembers his father in a way Annabeth cannot. Please do not be hurt if he does not. Clearly he admires you a great deal.'

'I wonder, Clara... But no, never mind. Let's enjoy the lambs, shall we?'

'What do you wonder?'

Why had she touched his lips as if she were infatuated with them? If that was what he wondered, she would need to say that she was sorry, even if she was not...quite.

'What do *you* call me? In your heart, where no one can hear but you. You, like George, remember Spencer well.' He studied the straw scattered about the floor, as if afraid to look at her and see her expression. 'What do you call me?'

'I call you friend...and husband.'

He glanced up sharply.

'Andrew, I call you husband because that is who you are.'

'I only wondered if it was too soon...if Spencer was still...'

She shook her head. 'There might be moments when I have memories. But that is all they will be, recalled and then put away. You must understand that I am not like your mother, mourning forever. Lost love is just that. Cherished and fondly remembered but not endlessly grieved over. Just because I have had my one true love, it does not mean we cannot have a perfectly friendly marriage. There is no ghost lurking between us.'

And then she did it. She kissed him…lightly, playfully.

'You see? Now we shall speak no more of it. I am anxious to hold a lamb.'

She stood up, walked to the pen, then bent to pluck up a fuzzy bleating creature. She pressed it to her bosom and rocked it the same way she would a baby. She cooed into the flicking ear.

The motion bought to mind the child she had lost one week after she'd discovered it existed…one week after she'd buried Spencer.

Perhaps one day…

'Clara, no matter my reasons for marrying, I think of you as my wife. Wife and dear friend. I have no regrets.'

Well, then…yes, perhaps.

If anyone had told Clara she would be content living in the country, she would have argued it to be unlikely. She was a city lady, born and raised in the loveliest parts of London.

However, to her surprise, the loveliest parts of London did not compare to a simple country meadow. There was no place in the city where she could walk alone. Even in Mayfair a lady required a companion to go out.

But just now she was walking quite safely across a meadow in the company of the sweetest of companions.

'Papa says there is a pond over there. May we go and see, Mama?' Annabeth asked.

The purpose of their outing was to give Annabeth fresh air and exercise. Dr Turner had said this was important, so that her daughter would not become ill again.

'As long as it is not too far away.'

This was their first outing, and Clara thought it best not to overtax her.

Reaching the top of a low hill, on the other side of which Annabeth believed there to be a pond, she realised her daughter was already overtaxed.

But her child was insistent upon going all the way to the pond.

It was not so far off—only at the bottom of the hill. It would be no difficult task to carry her down.

'It does look an engaging place to rest for a while,' said Clara. And for Annabeth to catch her breath.

'I'll chase the ducks.'

Clearly they had different expectations of what they might do at the charming pond.

A rest under the shady trees growing all about seemed ideal to Clara. Racing after water fowl appealed to her daughter, although her health was not recovered enough for it.

Clara thought her child took after her in temperament. Annabeth did like getting her way.

'Very well. We shall both chase ducks and then we shall both take a restful nap in the shade.'

She scooped her daughter up and started down the hill.

'Run, Mama, before they fly off.'

'If I run I will frighten them away.'

They were only yards from the ducks when she set Annabeth down. The ducks did not seem to care that they were being crept up upon, one slow step at a time.

'Ready?' she whispered.

Annabeth released her hand, gave a great whoop, then launched herself at the birds.

Clara followed. It felt rather joyous to whoop and leap about. If one acted this way in Hyde Park it would raise eyebrows, cause laughter.

Oddly the birds did not seem all that frightened.

They simply waddled to the water's edge, then glided away over the surface.

'May we watch them swim?' asked Annabeth.

What she needed was a proper snooze under the lovely shady trees, but it could wait a few minutes. For now it was good to sit down on the grass and simply spend time together. When they'd lived in London Clara had had no time for anything but working, keeping everyone fed and housed.

For a while they commented on this funny duck and that graceful one. And within a few minutes her daughter curled up on her lap and fell asleep.

She had missed this sort of moment over the last two years more than she'd realised. Life had been too busy for these tender, special moments.

Seeing Annabeth relaxed made her sleepy too. Sliding down into the grass, she lay down, spooned her child close to her heart.

'Dear Lord,' she murmured as she drifted off. 'Thank you for sending Andrew to us...'

She'd meant only to doze lightly, but she must have slept.

An unusual scent brought her towards the surface of consciousness. Something moist was huffing in her face, snorting against her shoulder.

Oh, no... Slowly, she opened one eye.

She screamed and jumped to her feet, grabbing Annabeth up with her.

She screeched again. And who would not, having a pair of huge brown bovine eyes staring at her?

The beast lashed its tail back and forth.

'Go away!' she yelled.

The bull bellowed, pawed the ground, set its posture to lunge.

With a great shove, she pushed Annabeth onto a low tree limb. 'Climb!'

Her daughter had never climbed a tree, but with a cry she scrambled up, as quick and agile as a boy. Clara had never climbed a tree either, and was certain she would not be quick, certainly not agile.

Nothing in her past had prepared her for facing off with a bull. The smelly animal was as tall as she was and hundreds of pounds heavier, and it made a deep sound—something between a growl and a bellow. The ground shook when it pawed at it again and again.

She circled the tree, placing the trunk between them. The bull did not follow but held its place, head lowered and eyes set on her every move.

Glancing up, she saw Annabeth high in the branches. 'Come up, Mama!'

Could she? Skirts and inexperience would not be in her favour. Neither would running away. If she got trampled, what would become of her child? She would be stranded in a tree, that is what!

Clara made a leap for the branch she had tossed Annabeth onto. Pulling and grunting, she managed to loop one leg over the branch.

The bull lunged. She heard her skirt tear, felt the tug of what had to be its horn. Some other part of the animal bumped her leg in the instant before she got her knee over the branch.

Pure terror shot her the rest of the way up the tree.

Looking down, she saw the bull trotting away—but not far enough.

At least they were safe up here. Bulls, she was certain, did not climb.

But then… Oh, mercy! What they *did* do was charge…at tree trunks.

It charged.

The trunk shook with the force of impact. It swayed. She gripped her daughter with one arm and a branch with the other.

'Ho!' a distant voice shouted. 'Ho!'

'It's Papa,' Annabeth cried.

Beyond reason, there he was, running down the hill, waving his arms at the bull.

Oh, no! The animal would surely charge Andrew next, crush him.

Andrew stopped running several paces from the tree and the bull. 'Go home, Thor.'

Thor?

With a long bellow, the bull turned about, plodded off to wherever he must have come from…home, was it? Or the underworld?

Andrew stood at the base of the tree, looking up.

And then he started to laugh.

Of all the outrageous reactions to the danger they had been in!

It was unacceptable—that was what it was.

'What is wrong with you, Andrew Benton? We might have been maimed!'

He bent over, and with his hands on his knees laughed harder. 'It is quite safe,' he said with a broad grin, once he had gained control over his guffaws. 'You may come down.'

Rudely, he wiped tears of mirth on his sleeve.

What could he find funny about barely escaping the beast's rage?

'What did you do to get Thor so annoyed?'

'Mama screamed.'

Apparently Annabeth had got over her fright as soon as she saw Andrew.

'Ah, that would do it. Poor old Thor is frightened of screams.'

'Is he, now? I would suggest he not come upon sleeping people and huff in their faces, then.'

'Come down and you can advise him of that.'

She really did not appreciate the humour lurking in her husband's eyes.

'He really is the gentlest of souls,' said Andrew. 'But he does tend to wander away from the home farm.'

'I would not get close to that vicious creature even if I could come down. Which I cannot.'

'You got up—come down the same way.'

'I got up under the threat of being mauled. The beast charged the tree and tried to shake us out. He ripped my skirt.'

'Or was it perhaps this vicious branch?' He plucked a piece of fabric from the branch, waved it at her.

'I saw the look in his eye. He meant to…' She should say no more. She did not wish to further frighten Annabeth who, as it turned out, was actually not as frightened as she was.

'You startled him, that's all. But he is gone now. Hand Annabeth down to me.' Andrew lifted his arms, waggled his fingers.

They were not up terribly high, would only have been just out of the reach of the beast's sharp horns, so it was easy enough to pass her down.

'May we visit Thor, Papa? Tell him we are sorry for screaming and scaring him?'

'No, we may not!'

Not under any circumstances, and no matter how much Andrew insisted that the bull was gentle, that he was the frightened one.

'Come down, Clara. I will catch you,' he said.

Would he? She was no feather of a woman. More likely than not they would both end up sprawled on the ground.

'I will come down on my own.'

He shrugged, grinned. And then remained where he was as if he believed she would not manage.

Oh, she would show him!

She hoped.

It could not be as far to the ground as it seemed, surely.

Andrew lifted his arms. It was tempting to lean towards them and see what happened. But no. If she could keep her family safe in a slum, she could get herself out of a tree.

She shifted her weight to the left, but that felt awkward. She shifted it to the right, which seemed perilous. Turning, she faced the trunk, stared at the rough bark which was sure to scrape her nose. She reached for a branch with her toe, waved her foot. Nothing solid there.

Annabeth giggled, the small traitor.

When she thought it was hopeless, her shoe brushed

the branch. She eased her weight onto it. Looking down, she saw it was the last branch before the drop to the ground. With her arms wrapped tight around the trunk, she tried to inch down. But her legs dangled. She tried to swing them around the tree, but all that did was make her lose her grip.

Any second now she would fall and bruise her behind on the ground.

All she could hope for was not to embarrass herself by weeping.

Rather than facing a fall on the ground, she ought to have accepted Andrew's help. Now she was good and stuck. And far too proud to admit she was wrong.

Something touched her rump—and it was not hard earth.

'I've got you.'

Oh, mercy… His big hands supported her bottom. Very gently, he lowered her the rest of the way down.

There was no reason for her cheeks to be flaming. She was his wife, and in other circumstances he would be quite familiar with that part of her anatomy.

But they did not live in other circumstances, by their own choice.

'Forgive me, Clara, but you really were about to fall. I did not wish for you to be injured.'

No decent husband would. She understood the necessity. What she did not understand was why the heat of his palms lingered on her skin.

She knew, of course, his hand had not been on her skin. There had been yards of fabric between his hand and her flesh. Where the heat lingered was in her mind…which was so much worse.

'Of course. There is nothing to forgive.' Only a fool would think there was.

Once again Andrew had come to her aid. Which she did not mind, except that she was accustomed to coming to her own aid.

Her husband had the most peculiar look on his face—at least it was peculiar for him. It was not as if she had never seen the like before. Spencer had used to look that way when he was thinking about bedding her.

Surely, though, she was mistaken about what was on Andrew's mind.

'Andrew, why are you looking at me that way?'

Asking was the only way to know.

'I am relieved you were not hurt in a fall.'

He might be relieved, but that was not the look he was suddenly trying to hide from her.

'Or by the bull,' she pointed out.

'Thor wouldn't hurt us, Mama.' Annabeth tugged on her skirt to get her attention. 'May I keep this duck?'

Her gazed jerked down at Annabeth at the same time as Andrew's did. She clutched a duck to her heart, smiling quite happily over it.

'No!' she and Andrew spoke in unison.

'How did you manage to pick it up?' Andrew asked.

And why wasn't it struggling to get away? wondered Clara.

'I told him I was his friend.'

'Still, it must remain here, where it belongs, with its friends and its pond.'

'It will miss me.'

If only tears had not been welling in the child's eyes, it would be easier to refuse her.

'We will visit often,' Andrew said. 'Would you like that?'

'Will Thor come and visit too?'

'We can only hope not,' she declared.

'But, Mama, I will tell him I am his friend too.'

Andrew laughed. 'If it is all right with your mother, I will bring you to visit the duck. I told Thor we were his friends long ago.'

'Is that all it takes? To declare you are his friend?'

If that was true, what would happen if she declared she and her husband would be lovers? She had to wonder, because his hands had been upon her person in a way which would…

Nothing.

An agreement was an agreement, and so far there was nothing to indicate he had changed his mind about it.

Almost nothing...

There had been that look. She knew very well what had been behind it. The feeling might have been fleeting, maybe even regretted, but she had seen what she had seen. And, having seen it, she hardly knew what to think.

Given she had entered this marriage with no expectation of intimacy, she did not feel that it betrayed Spencer. And why would it? She was no longer in mourning for Spencer—had put her grief behind her.

But her loyalty to him in the bedroom...that was a bit trickier than grief. She had never been with another man...

In the end she was stressing herself over something that did not matter. Andrew did not want her in his bed. She was not likely to betray Spencer in that way. Only, she did like Andrew. Was starting to have feelings that went beyond friendship.

'Look at those clouds,' she said, noticing a black mass roiling on the horizon. 'Things are changing.'

And that last comment had not a thing to do with the weather.

After several weeks of marriage, things were going well, in Andrew's opinion. Life was falling satisfyingly into place.

His mother was happier than he had ever seen her.

She had told everyone from the upstairs maids to the scullery maids that she could not wait for more grand-children to come into the family.

They would not be coming, but he found it impossible to tell her so. Luckily, Annabeth and George kept her smiling.

His mother was delighted to be called Grandmother.

He was charmed when Annabeth called him Papa.

Lilly was happy. She was the proud possessor of two wardrobes full of gowns, and even had a few suitors to show off her gowns to.

Annabeth was healthy. Clara vowed it had been a long time since she had seen her with such a sparkle in her eyes, so much happy energy in her step.

George's favourite thing to do was spend time on the farm with Bosing and the animals, which was a good, healthy occupation. However, it was now time he became enrolled in a proper school. There were a few nearby, but more in London.

Which was one of the reasons that this warm, sunny morning found him and Clara aboard a train, chugging towards the city. He had business to conduct during their stay there, but they would also look at schools for George.

Andrew looked forward to showing Clara a bit of fun. It had been years since she'd had the pleasure of attending the opera or the theatre. And, even though his cook was superb, he meant to take his wife to some of London's finest eating establishments so that she could wear her new gowns. To Andrew's way of thinking, it had been too long since she'd enjoyed the life she had been born to.

The train ride from the village to London was short. Not even two hours. Conversation between them never lagged. It was always interesting. They spoke often of the children, who day by day, felt more a joy than a responsibility.

'I have plans for our evenings in London, Clara, but I hope you will be able to find something to do in the mornings. You will enjoy being pampered by the staff, I trust. You deserve it after what you have been through in the past couple of years.'

'Truly, Andrew, being pampered seems a frivolous waste of time. What will you be doing in the mornings? I believe I will be far more interested in that.'

'Tomorrow I will visit one of my ships which is in port,' he said. 'But there are several shops in town which might interest you.'

'I'm sure I have frequented them all in the past. The last thing I require is a new gown.'

'A new pair of boots? A shawl? A bonnet?'

'If you find shopping so stimulating, perhaps you should accompany me?'

That sounded like a form of torture. Men conducted business and ladies shopped. It was the way of society.

'I see from your frown that you do not wish to explore the shops any more than I do.'

Her smile was pure provocation...the way she arched her brows and tilted her head. Charming, certainly, but defiant as well.

'I shall accompany you to the ship.'

That would not do. A ship with its crew of rough sailors was no place for a woman.

'Many sailors are superstitious about having a woman aboard.'

'Indeed? Well, I promise not to bring them bad luck.'

'That is not the point. They will believe it. Anything that goes wrong will be blamed on you. I cannot have my employees resigning.'

'That is unenlightened. Once they discover nothing awful has happened because I walked their decks for a brief time they will be the better for it.'

They would not. What he needed was to involve her in something else.

'Look, Clara, even though I am enlightened, and do not believe you would bring bad luck, I cannot allow it.'

'How enlightened can you really be, then, to take

the side of a warped notion rather than the common sense of your own wife?'

Was this their first disagreement as man and wife? It seemed to be leading that way.

'I have an idea,' he said, since a compromise was clearly called for. 'I have business at the former Albright factory tomorrow. Perhaps you would accompany me there?'

The train's whistle screeched, announcing their arrival in London.

The frown and the way she bit her bottom lip was not encouraging. But, standing, she plucked and smoothed her skirts into order.

'That will do.'

Would it? He could not help but think he had made a mistake in presenting the offer. Memories were bound to come up. Good and bad, he supposed. No doubt she would see her late husband in every corner of the place. That might account for her first, seemingly reluctant, reaction to the invitation.

He could hardly withdraw it now.

What he would do was make certain her attention was occupied with accounts, with fabrics and…

Anything but on Spencer Albright.

For her sake only.

Not for the way it made him feel—which was something akin to…not jealousy, but something uncomfortably like it.

How odd that he should feel anything at all, since he was not in love with her…

The next afternoon Clara and Andrew rode towards the factory in the comfort and security of his carriage. Even now, she could scarcely believe the turn her life had taken.

Going past the Ragged School, Clara looked out of the window. She felt heartsick, seeing the conditions of the children coming out through the front door. Still, they were luckier than some of the poor children in London. A great deal of praise was due those people who taught the children here. It must feel an impossible task to teach them what they needed to learn in order to rise from the poverty which seemed so natural to them.

If not for Andrew, George would still be among these children…or perhaps not if he'd run off to labour his youth away.

'What are you thinking, Clara?' Andrew asked.

'About the difference in the schools we looked at this morning and this one.'

'Whatever school we choose for George, it will have the best staff that money can buy.'

'And I am grateful. But I cannot think they will be any more dedicated than the instructors at this school. These teachers come every day and fight for poor children's futures. I know how poverty digs into one's soul until the day's survival is all life is about.'

'You do not need to be afraid. You will never be in that place again.'

She might be. Unless she had a hand in Andrew's accounts a tragedy could land her right back where she was.

But it would do no good to tell him so. Her husband was set on the fact that it was men who should be in charge of money. And there was nothing she could do about it.

The carriage stopped at the factory. Her heart jolted. She had not been inside this building in four years or more. Even from the outside, during her trips to the fish vendor, she'd been able to see that it had changed—and not for the better. She'd used to watch the employees leaving for the day. There had been no joy in their step, only weariness.

Stepping down from the carriage, she spotted the fish vendor across the street.

'I need a moment, Andrew. I shall meet you inside.'

'You should not be alone. I will wait for you here.'

'Really, Andrew, I spent two years walking this very street alone.'

'I can do nothing about what you had to do before. But right now there is a seedy-looking fellow in that doorway over there who has an eye you. He'll rob you of your very shoes if given the chance. I will be here.'

He was not wrong. She had to admit it. And there was probably more than one thief giving the carriage a sidelong glance.

It was hard to forget those nights when she had hugged her basket tight under her arm for fear that her fish would be taken.

Giving her husband a nod, she crossed the street to the vendor's stall.

At once Mr Horton looked away from the customer he was speaking with.

'Is there something I can help you with, my lady?'

'A moment of your time only—when you are finished with your customer.'

He hurried through the transaction, then returned his attention to her.

'Do you know who I am?' she asked.

'I'm sure I have not had the pleasure.'

'You first knew me as Mrs Albright. My husband owned the factory across the street.'

'Oh, my, yes! My apologies. How could I forget?'

'But do you remember me…without being dressed as I am?'

He looked at her, this way and that, then shook his head.

'Until very recently I haggled with you nearly every night for the best bargain on fish and potatoes.'

'Of course…for you and your children… I beg your pardon for not recognising you.'

'I would be surprised if you had. But I want to thank you for your kindness to me, sir. I was aware that you often gave me more than I paid for. And I would like to return the kindness.'

'There is no need. I get by well enough. But I am happy to see that your situation has improved.'

'I have married again.' She reached into her purse, withdrew a good sum of cash. 'What I would like is to help you do for others what you did for me. Please accept this for the extra you might give them. And please do keep some—do something for your family. I will always remember your kindness. Truly, Mr Horton, I do not know how my family would have survived without your charity.'

With that, she turned back to Andrew, who stood by the carriage wheel, his gaze shifting up and down the street.

'Mr Horton was kind to me before,' she explained.

'Shall we go inside? I believe the owner is waiting for us.'

'I only met him once. After I lost everything, and the factory was sold, I paid a visit. It was merely sentimental on my part, and I do not think he was pleased to see me. But at one time I…" She pressed her fingertips on his sleeve while they mounted the interior steps to the offices. 'I imagine he will be less pleased to see me now.'

'Why would he be?'

'I wish to discover how the employees are faring. I established a clinic, here in the building. For those injured on the job, and also for those who were not feeling well. And I maintained a shop here, stocked with garments which did not sell, asking only a pittance for them. The employees are the ones to have sewn those garments, after all.'

'You will be even more sympathetic to their labours now, I expect, having done it yourself.'

'Sympathy is all I have to offer, Andrew. The new owner can treat his people as he pleases, with no one to argue.'

Entering a waiting room, they were greeted by an unsmiling secretary who escorted them into Mr Smith's office.

'Good day, sir,' Mr Smith said to Andrew. 'And Mrs Albright—what a surprise.'

Not a happy surprise, she would wager, judging by the sour look on his face. She did not take it terribly to heart, since she knew him to be sour with nearly everyone.

'Mrs Benton, now," she corrected. "How pleasant to see you again.'

Andrew placed his hand on her shoulder, gave it a reassuring squeeze.

'Ah, Mrs Benton... I cannot imagine how I will entertain you while your husband and I conduct our business. I am afraid we are not equipped to entertain visiting ladies.'

Hmph! When she had had a hand in affairs there had been tea for visitors and the ladies had always enjoyed touring the place where their garments were made.

'No matter. I will be happy enough watching all that goes into you purchasing your goods.' She gave Mr Smith an engaging smile but, as she'd thought, it did not hit the mark. Apparently she would have to get what she wanted of this meeting by wit and not charm. 'I shall sit beside you and absorb everything you and my husband say to one another. Will you write everything down? Or will you simply shake hands on your transactions?'

Andrew gave her a look, while taking a chair at the large office desk. She had special memories of this desk but neither of these men with their hands folded upon it would appreciate knowing what they were.

Clara took a chair, moved it close to Mr Smith's elbow. So close that his arm would knock hers whenever he moved. Sometimes when he did not. Naturally she had a dozen questions which had little to do with the transaction at hand.

Bless Andrew for going along with her, for smiling indulgently no matter what inane thing she said. He would understand that she wished to explore but would never be invited to.

When the time came for her to excuse herself, to use the facilities, Mr Smith was good and ready to see her leave.

The first place she wished to visit was the clinic. She went down the office staircase. At the bottom she turned right, down a long corridor. It was dark and damp. In the past there had been lamps and landscape paintings on the walls.

She came to the door where the clinic had been and found it locked.

What happened when an employee cut herself? It was not unheard of in a clothing factory.

Hopefully the employee shop was still operating. There was no reason it should not be. Unlike the clinic, which required a nurse, it only needed a spare room, with a basket for people to leave money for their purchases.

Clara walked four doors down from the clinic. No shop in sight.

Surely the nursery that mothers had brought their babies and toddlers to while they worked was still in operation? That had been here since before Spencer had purchased the building.

She heard the hum of sewing machines and opened the door to find at least fifty seamstresses bending over their machines.

Even the light was dimmer than it had been.

The place was nothing like she remembered.

Clara wanted to weep.

In the past women would be laughing and telling stories while they worked. Once in a while someone would sing and others would join in.

What had happened to make them so sombre?

If anyone noticed her come in, or recognised her from before, they did not look up to greet her. No, there was not even a glance of curiosity for their visitor. The only noise besides the rustle of fabric and the hum of the machines was the tapping of her shoes on the floor.

A moment later another door opened and a stern-looking woman strode into the workroom. Clara stepped into a deep shadow. She wished to observe and perhaps discover what was making the ladies so glum.

The reason could be the woman now walking up and down the rows of ladies busy at their machines. Dressed in grey, her tall, thin figure was straight as a rod. She held a stick in her hand which she tapped on her palm.

She stopped to peer over the shoulder of a worker, slapped the rod on the sewing table. 'You are lagging, Edith. Pick up your pace or your pay will be docked.'

Slap, slap, slap went the stick on her palm. *Clink, clink, clink* went a set of keys hanging from her belt when she walked.

This was intolerable...the factory used to be a good place for a woman to work. But now...?

Clara stepped into the light, feeling as outraged as she ever had.

'Who are you? How did you get in here?'

Clara approached the woman, lifted her brows and gave her a stern glare. 'Mrs Clara Albright Benton.' She used all the names in case this 'guard' recognised one of them. 'I am familiar with every door and corridor so it was easy enough.'

'Visitors are not allowed.'

Visitor? What she was, was a spy...an investigator.

'I am certain that if you check upstairs in the office you will find I am permitted to be here.' She was not certain, but while the woman went to check Clara would have time to speak with the ladies, perhaps reunite with any of the old employees who remained.

'Wait in here.' Mrs Glum Face pointed the way down the corridor with her stick.

Clara was led to a room a short distance from the sewing room.

Very well, she would wait there—but only until the guard went upstairs. Once she was gone, Clara would come out and speak with the ladies.

The room turned out to be a cupboard, with no proper place to sit down. Bolts of fabric were stacked along two walls. Buckets for cleaning and wet mops along another wall.

No reputable clothing manufacturer would keep mops and fabric in the same room.

While she mentally berated Mr Smith for his slovenliness, as well as his disregard for the welfare of his employees, the door was closed on her. A key scratched in the lock.

Blazing mercy! She was trapped in a windowless room so dark she could not see up from down.

She pounded on the door, doubting that anyone would hear. Even if they did, they were not likely to help her. Surely any who did would lose her employment. Rescuing her from imprisonment in a cupboard would not be worth risking her family's financial security.

The floor smelled dirty. Since she had no idea how long she would be in here while the miserable woman went upstairs, or if she even was really doing so, she would need to make herself comfortable.

Feeling the back wall, she ran her fingers over the bolts of fabric. Hmm... Not wool, too scratchy. Not brocade or homespun. Ah, velvet...that would do nicely.

She wondered what colour she was making a nest of. Red, she decided. It was a good warm colour, and it was quickly becoming cold in the cupboard.

Since it was impossible to see anyway, she closed her eyes. If she managed to fall asleep she might not think too deeply on the fact that she was probably not alone in here. Rats in factory cupboards were not uncommon.

Except for the cold, the dampness and the fear of an unwelcome companion, she was in no real danger.

'Andrew will come for me,' she muttered.

As soon as his business was finished, he would come looking. Mr Smith and his lady minion would be the ones in trouble then. And it served them right.

Clara settled into the yards of velvet plumped about her. She kept her mind busy with images of Andrew lashing Mr Smith with a few choice words. It was nice knowing someone was watching out for her. For so long it had been her watching out for everyone else, the responsibility for their wellbeing lying squarely on her shoulders.

And then Andrew had knocked on her door. After that, everything had changed.

Oh, she had fought him, thinking perhaps he was mad. But he'd persisted, and praise the Good Lord that he had.

Brr... It was getting cold in here. But even though she was beginning to shiver, she did not fear freezing to death.

Andrew was coming.

Andrew did not expect Clara to return from using the facilities right away. He understood that had been an excuse to look around. He even lingered over the transactions he was conducting in order to give her more time.

At one point this factory had been important to her. She needed to put that part of her life to rest in order to move on. He believed that.

He was beginning to worry, though. She had been gone much longer than he'd expected. Even accounting for her stopping to chat with former acquaintances she had been gone a long time.

An hour ought to have been plenty of time and it was now approaching ninety minutes. He knew the number of minutes because he had been watching the clock tick them off.

A tall woman dressed in grey poked her head into the office. 'May I have a word, Mr Smith?'

With a nod Smith excused himself and went into

the other room. When he closed the door it creaked back open an inch.

'There is a woman downstairs. I have a bad feeling about the chit. Nosy as the dickens and trying to spy on us, I would wager. I have put her away until you have time to deal with her.'

Through the crack Andrew saw the woman tapping her palm with a thin stick. The rhythmic pattern of wood on flesh was unnerving. 'She has had an hour to think things over.'

'Well done, Mrs Martin,' Smith whispered. 'I guessed she was—'

Andrew leapt out of his chair. Shoved the door open. 'What have you done with my wife?'

'Your *wife*?' the woman made a strange growling, sneering noise in her throat. 'You ought to keep a tighter leash on the woman, if you ask me. She was annoying the workers.'

'Take me to her at once.'

He pushed past them, no matter that the grey ghoul knew the way and he did not.

She managed to get ahead of him at the foot of the stairs, then led him through a work area and into a corridor. Out of breath, the woman stopped in front of a cupboard door.

'If you have put my wife in a cupboard you will regret it.'

His voice sounded too mild for the anger raging in him, flaming at the very limits of his temper.

That was what they were standing in front of, however. A blighted, blasted closet!

The woman jangled her keys. Her hand trembled when she put one in the lock and turned it.

Light spilled into the dank and smelly space.

Lying on the floor, in a great cloud of various colours of velvet, lay Clara—asleep, with one hand tucked under her cheek.

And shivering.

Pivoting on his heel, he turned slowly. Balling his fist, he meant to plough it into Smith's jutting, arrogant chin. No matter that he had not been the one to put Clara in the closet, he'd seemed to condone it.

He swung his arm. But at the last second his father's teaching about charity and patience came to the man's rescue. Andrew's fingers barely whispered against Smith's face.

Still… All that anger needed a place to go. He snatched Smith's collar, drew him up to his toes, then yanked him close, until they were nearly nose to nose.

'Find another supplier—if you can. Our association is ended.'

Shoving him backwards, he watched the man trip over his own shoes. He ploughed into the grey ghoul and they both went down.

Stepping into the closet, Andrew crouched beside his wife, touched her cheek gently to wake her. Her skin was cold, which made him even angrier.

'Clara?'

Her eyes fluttered open. She smiled at him. 'I knew you would come, Andrew. You always come,' she murmured sleepily.

'That is something you may count on, Clara. I always will come.'

He helped her up with an arm about her waist. Then he kept it there.

'Did you punch them?' she asked. 'Please say you did.'

The pair in question were rolling about on the floor, trying to untangle themselves from one another.

'Nearly. Then I remembered I am the son of a minister.'

'But something has happened to them,' she said as they walked past.

'It has. When I let go of Smith's collar I might have shoved him a bit harder than a minister's son ought to. He crashed against that ghoul woman. Then over they went. You must be so cold...'

'I was, but not anymore. Andrew, as a minister's son, are you allowed to call a lady a ghoul?'

'I would never call a *lady* a ghoul, so you may make what you like of it.'

She snuggled close, and looked up at him in admiration. There was no denying it made him feel rather grand to be looked at as her hero.

'Wicked. That is what she is. If you only saw how she treats the poor women who work here.' She stopped, went up on her toes and kissed his cheek. 'Had you hit them it would have been understandable. I would have applauded you.'

'Let's go home, where you can sing my praises.'

Walking beside him as they left the building, she laughed. 'If applause is not enough, the best I can do is hum your praises.'

'Perhaps we should simply have dinner,' he said, handing her up into the carriage. 'We shall dine in tonight, if you do not mind. There has been enough adventure for the day.'

Instead of taking the spot across from him she sat beside him on the bench, snuggled in. 'You are so warm, Andrew.'

He *was* warm. Even though the flush of anger was fading, he felt like loosening his collar, unbuttoning his shirt. This was a unique sort of heat. One he had not felt so strongly before—not even for the lovely Edna Powers.

It was also one he did not particularly welcome.

Lust had no place in friendship. He would do well to remember it.

His affection for his wife was growing deeper every

day. But he reminded himself that he had no wish to end up broken-hearted as his mother had...twice. Nor did he wish for Clara to end up broken-hearted either.

For both their sakes he would refrain from giving in to lust.

Which meant that now...when she was lifting her face to him, setting her smile and her lips just so for a kiss...he was just going to tap those lips with his finger. Playfully...in a frolicsome gesture of misunderstanding what he knew she wanted.

'I wonder what Cook has planned for this evening?'

What food would pass over those pretty, expectant lips?

He swiped a finger between his collar and his neck in an attempt to let out a little of the building steam.

'Indeed,' she said, then slid away from him. 'Something hot and simmering, I imagine.'

'Perhaps with some bread...and butter, I think.'

'Not *melted* butter.' She crossed her arms over her middle. 'If you wish for bread and butter that is what you shall have.'

She cast him a sidelong glance which told him she would not be humming his praises tonight after all.

With spring setting in, roses of every hue bloomed in the garden.

Clara and her mother-in-law strolled along the stone

path admiring the bright colours and fresh scents. Unlike her garden in Mayfair, which had been contained by walls, this garden had no gate, but rather a view of lush rolling hills, hedges and trees.

Sheep and their young lambs dotted the hills.

Luckily, Thor was nowhere to be seen.

'I am bursting to know, my dear,' her mother-in-law said, quite out of nowhere.

'What is it, Mother? Perhaps I have an answer.'

'You are the only one who knows.' Mrs Benton winked. 'When we can expect a little Andrew to make an appearance, of course.'

'Not yet.'

As matters stood, Baby Andrew might never make an appearance. Not if her husband did not even wish to kiss her.

'In the Good Lord's time, Mother,' she said.

It seemed a little divine intervention might be in order, because her husband had made it clear from the beginning that he did not wish for romance between them.

She had agreed...then. Having had her one true love, she'd believed she needed no other. However, she was beginning to wonder if that attitude was irrational.

Many people had more than one true love. She had

not thought to be among them. But then Andrew had knocked upon her door and refused to be sent away.

'May I ask you a question, Mother?'

'But of course, my dear girl. I am nothing but a fount of information—in the subjects I am familiar with at any rate.'

'I hope it is not insensitive to bring this up, but Andrew has told me that when his father died you were certain you would never love again. And yet you did.'

'Yes, of course. What else could I do? Oh, if you had ever met Miles's father you would understand. He was the most charming of men. I could not cling to my broken heart once he began to court me. And my Miles is the image of his father. I cannot understand why some lucky lady has not snatched him up.'

Oh, he had been snatched up. But nothing would make Clara reveal that it had been in the tender embrace of the law.

Her mother-in-law's answer had not really helped. The poor woman had been blinded to the true character of the man who'd made her love again.

Clara knew very well who Andrew was. But she could not say she was in love with him. Nor could she say she was not developing a schoolgirlish crush.

How could she not after he'd rescued her from a

creepy cupboard and left a pair of villains floundering on the floor.

Andrew had come to her aid before, but that time his eyes had had heroic fire in them, and his hair had dipped across his forehead in a wild, ungentlemanly manner.

Which had made her heart flutter in a soft and curious way.

When they'd sat close together in the coach, she had wanted to kiss him. And not because she had been longing for kisses since her first husband had died... No, she had wanted Andrew's kiss and no other.

Not the sort she had taken in the past—quick friendly pecks done and forgotten. No, indeed. She had wanted him to wrap her up and take...take liberties, she supposed. Except they were married, so it would not have been liberties so much as something perfectly acceptable—expected, in fact.

'Oh, look, Clara! Here is the prettiest red rose. It is a sign, don't you think?'

'Of what, Mother?'

'True love's passion, of course. Here we are, speaking of it, and a symbol is right in front of us.' Mrs Benton picked the deep red flower and put it in the buttonhole of Clara's blouse. 'There, now. All will be well. You will see. Never fear, we will hold our little Andrew in our arms yet.'

* * *

Late that night, Clara sat in the chair beside her window, looking out at the moonlit landscape.

A large figure ambled along the crest of the hill to the west. Thor. Where was the beast going? What could he want in the deep of night?

The only thing she could think of that would bring him away from his nice warm stall was a cow. In his constant wandering, it seemed that the bull went to great efforts to woo his ladies and ensure there would be calves next season.

How interesting that cows tended to have a season for giving birth. If humans had one, Clara thought she must have missed a couple of seasons. With Annabeth now five years old, she might have had two more children by now had her life been different.

After Spencer's death she hadn't given too much thought about having another child. As a widow not intending to fall in love again, babies had not been first in her mind.

Until she'd married Andrew.

Watching Thor's dark, hulking figure plod towards what she thought to be his goal, she knew that love was not a part of his mission.

Children often came into the world without their parents being in romantic love. As long as they were committed as a family, and to the child's wellbeing, romance was not essential.

But then… Oh, when she thought back to how it had been when Annabeth had been born and how she and Spencer had been as infatuated with her as they had with each other…it had been wonderful.

But it did not, in the end, determine how much she loved her daughter. That was something quite apart. Her son had come to her under a completely different circumstance. Georgie was another woman's baby, but once Clara held him, she'd been as smitten as if she had given birth to him.

'You have the right of it, Thor,' she said aloud. 'Romance is between a man and a woman. Love between parents and children is a different love all together. I wonder if you even recognise your offspring once they are born.'

Watching him trek slowly along in the moonlight, she thought it was not likely. What *was* likely was that she was going to speak to Andrew in the morning. It was only right that, as her husband, he knew what was on her mind. It was not as if anyone else could give a baby Andrew to the family.

Not only that, the prospect of the act of conception was occupying her mind. Looking at her husband walking about each day, seeing how his muscles moved and shifted, watching his expressions when he smiled and when he frowned… The fact of the matter was, she was not inexperienced when it came to understanding her body's response to a man. The surprise was that it was responding at all. After Spencer she had not thought it possible.

Which only went to prove that Thor had the right of it.

Love and passion could act independently of one another.

Indeed, she was not in a full romantic tizzy over her husband, but the prospect of sharing his bed was making her feel warm and tingly.

And tomorrow she would make her feelings on the matter known.

'We will no longer conduct business with Frederick Smith,' Andrew told his accountant, as they faced each other across his wide office desk.

'I have heard unflattering things about him,' Joseph Billings said, and nodded while he put away his pens and closed the ledger. 'It is not the same factory as when Spencer Albright owned it. I believe you have made a wise choice in cutting ties.'

Andrew did not reveal why he was cutting ties. His reasons were personal more than business, and he wished to keep them private.

'I will see you next week, Mr Benton.' Joseph stood

to take his leave, nodded again, then walked across the office. He paused at the door before going out. 'Is there any word of your brother?'

'From what I hear, he is behaving himself. Quite the model prisoner.'

'As much as I dislike speaking ill of your relative, I almost wish he would act as who he really is and they would keep him longer.'

'As much as I dislike agreeing with you, I do.'

With one more nod, Joseph went out, closing the door behind him.

Andrew heard voices murmuring in the corridor. A moment later the office door opened and Clara came in. Seeing her always made him smile. Truly, she was everything he could have hoped for in a wife…no, she was more.

Whenever he came upon her, or she came upon him, he felt content. He had gained so much more from going into this marriage than he had expected to. Somewhere along the way Clara had gone from being a wrong to be set right, to a friend. A cherished friend.

Seeing her smile, and the way she sat down so comfortably across from him, he believed he would marry her a dozen times over. With their common expectations, no wife could suit him more perfectly.

'After spending three hours looking at numbers,' he said. 'It is a relief to see your smile, Clara.'

'After spending all day wishing I was in here with you, it is good to at least be sitting at the desk where numbers were being discussed.'

As well suited as they were, this was one matter they seemed to have difficulty finding agreement on.

'I have informed Billings we will no longer do business with Smith.'

'Mr Smith is not fit to run a business. I would have told him as much had I been allowed to dabble one finger in the sale of the factory.'

'Perhaps one day women will—'

She waved her hand between them, as if sweeping away his attempt to placate her. She believed what she believed, so any words would be useless anyway.

'There is something I wish to discuss with you, Andrew,' she said. 'It has nothing to do with business. It is a private matter…quite personal.'

'I hope you know you can come to me with anything. We have become more than casual friends, haven't we?'

'Much more, I think.' She stretched across the desk, took both of his hands in both of hers. 'And because we are more, there is something I wish to discuss with you.'

'I am all ears. What is it?'

'Well, you see… To come to the point…'

Funny how she looked so nervous, blushing as pink as a rose. Looking pretty with it, too.

'You are far more than ears,' she said. The blush had gone deep red. 'Which, actually, has to do with the reason I am here in your office.'

He squeezed her hands. 'Clara, my dear, you may trust me with anything you wish to tell me.'

'That is a relief.' She stood up, walked around the desk, and then sat down on his lap.

Her weight settled pleasantly down on him. She must not be aware of exactly how pleasant. Her small shifting, squirming movements made the blood drain from his brain, made it plunge to an inappropriate place, given the agreement they had about chastity in their marriage.

Surely she had no idea of what she was doing to him. He ought to tell her, but somehow did not want to. In a moment he would…but for just a little longer he would pretend they had made no such agreement, that their marriage was as normal as the next married couple's.

Although if they were a normal married couple he would not be so tormented in particular parts of his person.

'I am glad it is a relief,' he said. For her, but certainly not for him. 'What do you wish to tell me? If it is to do with finances, we just—'

'Oh, no.'

She brushed the hair away from his forehead. Hopefully she would not notice how he was beginning to sweat.

'It is something womanly, to be honest.'

'Now I am relieved.' Perhaps he was. But what he really was, was confused. What could she possibly be hedging around?

'Good… Very good, Andrew. Because what I want is a child.'

A what? He could not possibly have heard right.

'A baby? To adopt, you mean?'

'Do not play dense, Husband.' She stood up, her smile fading. 'I want a baby to give birth to.'

Dense, was it? His body had been understanding her message all along—it was only his brain having trouble keeping up.

'We did agree not to—'

'Fall in love.'

Standing, she gave him that stern look down her nose. It never failed to fascinate him, even in this surreal moment.

'You do understand that love is not required to conceive a child? The marital act can be accomplished without it.'

'What I do not understand is who you are in this

moment,' he said to her back, as she marched towards the door.

She went out, closed the door behind her...or perhaps slammed it. Seconds later it opened again.

'I am Mrs Andrew Benton.'

With that, she was gone.

He sat in his chair, as stunned as he had ever been.

What kind of man did she think he was? One who could lie with a woman...especially the one he was married to...and remain unmoved?

Could he? It seemed to him that Clara thought such a thing possible.

He had made it clear from the beginning that he did not wish to be moved. While she had made it clear that she already experienced her one true love.

Clara Benton was trying to change the rules—and he did not much care for it.

That conversation had gone miserably.

She had gone over it in her mind. Mentally reworded it all.

Over and over, she'd wondered what she could have said differently in order to convince him she was right. The matter was far too important simply to let it go.

Standing at her window, she watched the moonlight shiver on the meadow. Like last night, there went the intrepid Thor, on his way to create another calf.

At least that was what she'd attributed his nightly wanderings to. She did not know all that much about cattle, but she did not believe them to be nocturnal.

Clearly Thor did not live according to the rules.

The lady cows were probably quite surprised when he appeared in their meadow.

Perhaps that was what she ought to do—surprise her husband in his meadow...his chamber, as it were.

If she came upon him unawares perhaps his defences against her would be down.

Not that she would remain in his meadow if she was genuinely not wanted there...

As she saw it, Andrew did not actually know what he wanted. If she went to him and gave him a taste of what they could have, it might change his mind.

Having never been a father, he might not understand the joy a child would bring him. And she had reason to know the begetting of it would be pleasant.

Sitting on her chair, she drew her knees up to her chin, thinking about what she had in mind to do.

She was not Thor, for all that she was coming to admire the bull and his nightly outings. Her actions would have consequences.

Could she really lie with him and not fall in love?

Falling in love with him would be a betrayal of their understanding.

Truly, she did not know if she was ready to do it.

She plucked the rose which her mother-in-law had given her from its petite vase on the table next to the chair. The petals felt smooth when she drew them across her face, down her throat.

Mrs Benton believed the rose was a sign.

Between the sign of the rose and the inspiration of her mentor, Thor, she made her decision.

Nothing ventured, nothing gained, and all that.

She courted rejection, and that would be crushing. But at the same time she stood to gain something… someone…she had given up hope of having.

Andrew turned in his sleep…thought he'd heard something. After listening for a moment he decided he had not. He lapsed back into a dream which made little sense no matter how one looked at it. There was a task he was supposed to accomplish, but as hard as he tried he could not.

The oddest part was, he could smell a rose. The fragrance filled his senses until he thought it the most realistic dream he ever had. Something soft and velvety was touching the stubble on his chin. It glided across his eyelids and around the shell of his ear.

'Andrew…?'

The breath of a whisper took the place of the soft thing.

'Wake up, Husband.'

He opened one eye slowly, reluctantly. This was a far nicer dream he had drifted into than the other had been.

'Clara?'

The dream got nicer by the second. In his dream his wife was bent over his bed, holding a red rosebud. She was dressed in a cloud...pale blue, not white.

'Naturally it is me. Who else would be waking you in her shift with not even proper shoes on her feet?'

'Clara!'

Aware suddenly that this was no dream, he snapped open the other eye. His wife stood beside his bed, wearing something thinner than any cloud he had ever seen.

'Is something wrong?' he asked.

It must be urgent, otherwise she would have covered herself. Then again, urgency did not seem to fit the moment, since she had taken the time to tickle his face with a rose.

'Nothing is wrong... No, Andrew. This is so very right.'

She peeled the blanket back. A seductive smile lurked at the corners of her lips, lighting her eyes. He saw an invitation even in the dim light given off by the embers in the fireplace.

She sat on the bed, then slid down beside him without drawing the blanket over them.

'Are you cold?' he asked. 'Has your fire gone out?'

'I confess, it did for a while.'

She laid the rose on his chest, which was bare because that was how he slept. Then she touched his skin, circled her fingers over his heart.

'It is back now.'

'Clara, I—'

'Hush, now… There is something I wish to show you.'

'You are showing me quite a bit… Perhaps you ought to pull up the blanket.'

Or go back to your chamber.

That was what he ought to say, but could not quite. If he did, he might not discover what it was she wanted to show him. And he was as fascinated to know what it was as he was disinclined to.

'But it is my intention to show you.'

She snuggled close. Every part of him came to attention. Hot flaming attention.

'I have come to bare myself to you, Andrew…body and soul.'

He opened his mouth to say something. What it was he had no idea. It did not matter in the end, because she kissed him.

Strands of wispy hair tickled his chest. She touched his cheek, her fingers as smooth as the rose petals had been. Ah, but unlike the cool petals, her fingers sizzled.

Clara had a nice womanly swell from the dip of her waist to the fuller curve of her hip. He could not help but notice since he was touching that very swell.

He should not be… This was dangerous… He might as well be petting a viper. Or an angel. In his confused state he could not seem to distinguish one from the other.

'It is right for me to be here, Andrew.'

She was pressed so close to him that he could no longer feel the thin fabric of her gown. Just her. The nightgown served no purpose whatsoever…he might as well lift it off her.

The danger to them both was increasing with each breath, each racing heartbeat. Once they'd experienced this sort of intimacy they would be at risk for ever.

'Don't you see?' Her voice was a siren song, sweet and alluring. 'This is what marks the difference between marriage and friendship.'

'We agreed on friendship. We did not wish to risk our hearts.'

'I may have changed my mind.'

'Do not think that I am not tempted. You cannot have failed to notice. You are everything a man could want in a wife…in a lover. And yet I do not see how we can indulge without risking… But surely you know it would not be wise.'

'You are correct. It would not be wise.'

She left him. Got up from the bed and stood next to the window. Not that it helped his heated condition one whit to have her several feet away. Moonlight streamed in through the window, through her gown. He could see more of her now than he had while she was pressed against him in his bed.

At least it was now possible for him to keep his hands to himself. If one did not count what was going on in his imagination. That was still behaving in a way he did not fully approve of. Except that since he was the one imagining, he must be in some part approving.

'I will go back to my chamber in a moment,' she said. 'But there is something I must say first.'

He sat up, hung his legs over the edge of the bed and put his feet on the floor, drawing the blanket over his lower half for modesty.

Although, honestly, modesty had no part in this encounter.

'I have told you before that you may tell me anything, Clara.'

'And I intend to. However, you are not going to like it.'

Just now he no longer knew what he would like or not like.

'I came here tonight because I want a child. You know I do. The thing of it is, I believed we could accomplish the deed and have a lovely time doing it. But I was wrong.'

Not all wrong. It would have been a lovely time. Too lovely...

'It seems I am less like Thor than I would like to be.'

'Thor the bull?'

She nodded, pushed a hank of hair away from her face. 'He walks over the hill every night with the sole intention of creating calves. I thought I could do the same. But as it turns out I cannot lie with you and give you only my body.'

Her honesty robbed him of words...of the breath to speak them.

'I can only imagine what you must think of me,' she went on. 'Please believe that I decided before I came that if you were unwilling I would withdraw. Which, as you can see, I am doing.'

She gave a great sigh, revealing how much she regretted the need to withdraw.

'Clara, please understand... Were it for not the cost, I would not regret lying with you. But I have seen the price people pay for loving when they suffer loss.'

'Oh, you have seen it, have you?' She arched a fine, lovely brow at him, gave him an angry look. 'Let me tell you, Andrew Benton, I have *paid* the price. And I would not take back a single tear which was the cost of loving Spencer.'

'I am sorry. Of course you know that better than I do.'

Wasn't he an idiot of the first order not to have considered that? And he was about to become a worse one…

'I am sorry about the child you want, Clara. But I cannot lie with you simply to achieve it.'

'As it turns out, I cannot do it either.'

Her appearance had changed, her eyes gone soft. She was neither smiling nor frowning. What she looked was vulnerable.

'Perhaps with someone else I could, but not with you.'

Then, with a swish and a whisper of her filmy nightgown, she spun towards the door and left him sitting on the edge of his bed, holding his head in his palms while his brain whirled in confusion.

What had she meant by that?

Chapter Eight

A week after the failed seduction Clara decided to scrub a floor which did not need it. All she gained was raised brows from an upstairs maid. From there she moved to the kitchen, and pounded dough to make a loaf of bread.

The kitchen staff went about their duties, but they were clearly uncomfortable having her working among them.

She carried on anyway, because she needed something constructive to do.

The problem was, no matter what she did, she could not forget what a grand fool she had made of herself with Andrew.

As that grand fool, she had hinted that she was falling in love with him. While she had not said the words directly, he must have understood what she meant.

When she'd exited his room she had probably left him an unhappy man.

Unhappy and confused.

Declarations or hints of love were meant to be received in joy.

That was far from what had happened.

Partly because she had been stunned to make that particular discovery in that particular moment.

Having insisted she would never love again, and then discovering she was doing it, had left her shaken. And bewildered.

The change in her feelings had been gradual and disguised by their deepening friendship right up until the moment when she had lain beside her husband in his bed and they had blindsided her. She who had thought herself to be so knowledgeable in the ways of the marriage chamber.

She, of anyone, should have known she could not indulge in intimacy without being in love. It was only a shame she had not recognised the true state of her heart before she had crept, all but naked, into her husband's bed.

She would not have made such a fool of herself if she had.

And ever since the thwarted seduction and her hinted admission that she felt differently from the way that had been agreed upon, things had not been the same between them.

They were friendly enough, but lacking the ease which had once been between them.

She missed what they'd used to have. And now, days had gone by without a secret laugh or a joke which only they would understand.

Andrew went about the business of running his estate neither angry nor joyful. For all he'd had to say about the incident...her going to him and offering her body...and as it turned out her heart...had not even happened.

'Wretched man,' she muttered, while punching the bread dough.

Clara noticed the scullery maid and the cook exchanging glances. They would be relieved when she went back to the business of doing nothing constructive. To being a proper lady of the estate who occupied her time by entertaining. Which she did not do either, since they were keeping visitors away.

Perhaps she would sew a more modest sleeping gown, since she was unlikely to need, again, the one she had worn to seduce Andrew.

Heavy footsteps entered the kitchen.

'There you are,' Andrew said, giving a long glance to the dusting of flour covering her from wrist to elbow. 'I am going to London tomorrow, if you would like to go with me.'

'I would adore that,' she answered, not missing the relieved expressions on the faces of the kitchen staff.

Surely she would find something to do in London?

She dusted her hands on her apron, then handed over the dough to Cook.

'I fear you are getting bored in the country,' he said. 'Perhaps going to London will help.'

'Indeed… Perhaps having shops to visit will cure all my ills,' she answered.

Shopping would not do that, and he well knew it. However, she was not about to tell him—once again—what would.

She had agreed to the marriage they had. Just because she had changed her mind about it, it was not right to put the blame on him.

If the subject of love and marriage came up again, it would be from Andrew's lips. Until then she would find something else to occupy her time.

And it would need to be something interesting and worthy, because her husband seemed more and more desirable every time she looked at him.

And there was no way she could keep from looking at him.

Each time he smiled it went straight to her heart. And the sound of his voice, so rich and masculine, made her want to kiss him.

She simply must find something satisfying to do

with her time, or she would obsess over their lack of a proper erotic marriage.

A purpose was what she needed. Something noble to improve the lot of mankind.

Having a baby and raising it to be a responsible human being would do it, but apparently that was not to be.

And suddenly, right there in the corridor between the kitchen and the laundry, she knew what it was.

Tomorrow and London could not come soon enough.

For the past week Andrew had not felt himself.

He was not normally a maudlin fellow, but lately that was the way his thoughts tended.

Because of beliefs which he refused to budge from, he had turned away from his bed a woman who had every right to be there. His legally wedded wife of whom he was exceedingly fond.

Not only had he shunned a lady who would have made a tender, sizzling bed mate, but in the process he had turned away his best friend.

And now, although she was sitting across the dining table from him at his house in Mayfair, she seemed distant…preoccupied. It was as if in refusing her that night he had distanced her. And he had lost joy in the process. He would swear that when she had gone out of his chamber that night she'd taken it with her.

He missed hearing her laugh…missed, too, the spark that lit her green eyes when she was happy and when she was annoyed.

His wife wanted a child. He could understand that. But what he also understood was that women died in childbirth. He would have no part in risking her life that way.

Last time he and Clara had shared a meal at this table they'd understood each other well. Their ideas about marriage had been aligned. Life had been good.

Now something had shifted between them. The way he felt about life and the way she did, no longer meshed as nicely as threads woven into cloth.

And, after spending hours considering what she had told him that night, he was still confused.

Was it that, after being with him so briefly, so intimately, she had changed her mind about it being possible for her to couple for the sake of procreation and yet feel nothing?

Or, as it seemed, had she meant that about him in particular. That she could not be with him and not give him her heart?

Which was the very reason he had not taken what she'd offered. Had he done so, he would have had to surrender his heart.

But since they'd agreed on the matter it made no sense that they were now at odds.

There was one other possibility.

It was not that she feared having romantic feelings for him, but that she already had them.

In that moment he had thought it possible. With his body more aroused than it had ever been, and at the same time his heart tripping over itself, he had not been sure of anything.

He still was not—except for one thing. Being at odds with his wife was a situation he did not care for.

'Are you feeling ill, Andrew. You are not eating.'

'I am well, Clara, only preoccupied.'

While he knew they ought to speak about the reason for that, he would rather not scratch fresh wounds. Perhaps the easy way that had been between them would return on its own.

'What will you do with your morning?' he asked.

'I intend to keep busy. But I promise not to annoy the maids or the kitchen help.'

'I have business that will keep me in my office all day, but later we shall go to dinner—if that suits.'

'I would enjoy it.'

Standing, she walked around the table to where he sat. Looking down at him, she brushed away a strand of his hair which had flopped over one eyebrow. It was a wifely touch…the sort he would allow himself to enjoy.

'Andrew, there is something I must say.'

She drew in a deep breath, as if steadying herself for whatever it was.

'I apologise for coming into your chamber as I did. Knowing how you feel, I had no right to do it. I hope we can go back to being us…the way we used to be.'

She was braver than he was to bring it up. Left to himself, he would have let it be. Even though he knew wounds tended to fester that way.

'I have missed that.' He caught her hand, kissed it and found it did not feel odd, but natural. 'And I do regret that I cannot give you all you want.'

'You give me enough, Andrew. I am satisfied with our marriage.'

She smiled in the old way.

But, as relieved as he was to return the smile, he could not help but feel he was letting her down.

Her first husband had set an example of which he fell far short.

She bent at the waist, kissed his forehead with a demure, wifely kiss and then went out of the dining room.

Hopefully whatever she found to take up her day would be fulfilling, and help to make up for his failure as a husband.

Oddly, he had the curious sensation that Spencer Albright was frowning over his shoulder...

By the time the carriage arrived at the factory it was raining. Hinton drove as close as he could to the front door but, as she dashed for the building, Clara still got wet enough to leave drips of water on the stairway leading to the office.

Hardly a shame, that.

Coming inside the office, she told the receptionist that she wished to speak with Mr Smith.

This time, before the woman could dismiss her out of hand, the factory owner himself stepped into the reception area.

'Good day, Mrs Benton. May I be of service to you?'

His voice was as friendly as a sunny day. Perhaps he believed she had come to restore business ties with her husband. Let him think it, then.

'Bring us tea,' he instructed his receptionist, who gave him an arch glance in return.

Perhaps that was code between them for poison. When she had last been here she had destroyed several yards of velvet. Nonetheless, she was here on a mission and she would see it through.

When they were in his office, with tea set between them, she presented the reason for her visit.

'Mr Smith, when I was here last I noticed you have a large, empty room which seems to serve no purpose.'

'Business is slow, I am afraid. I cannot afford to keep it in use.'

'I completely understand. I recall the business having its ups and downs when my first husband owned the factory. Slow periods come from time to time.'

'I will be relieved when business picks up,' he stated, with a glance at the rain beating on the window.

'And I am certain it will. However, in the meantime it is a shame to see valuable space go to waste, don't you think?'

'There is no help for it.'

'I would like to make a suggestion. There is an excellent and worthy way in which you may put this space to use.'

'I assume you have come to ask for a resumption of business between your husband and myself?'

He tapped one finger on the desk—nervously or impatiently, she could not tell.

'I can only wonder why he sent you and did not come to do business with me himself.'

'Because I am not here on his business but my own.' When he looked at her in confusion, she pressed on, 'I propose you donate the space for a Ragged School.'

'Pray tell me, my lady, why would I do that?'

'Because children walk past your building every

day going to one that is three miles from here. It is not safe for them to do so. Surely you care about their wellbeing?'

He stood up, looking displeased, and sour as a lemon. 'You have wasted your time and mine,' he told her.

She stood, too. Having been turned down, the sooner she was on her way the better. This man was not to be trusted. But it in no way meant she would not return. Establishing a Ragged School was only one of the reforms she wished to discuss with him…

'I hope you will change your mind, Mr Smith. Those children need your help.'

'I offer employment to all, regardless of age. I do not know what better I can do. It is unlikely an education will do those children a bit of good, anyway. Good day to you.'

The rain which had come down steadily since that morning grew worse as the day wore on. Coming out of his office, Andrew was relieved to hear the front door close and his wife's voice drifting from the hall while she spoke briefly with Jones.

He met her in the hall, saw the smattering of raindrops on her lashes and whisked them away with his thumb. Doing it gave him the strongest urge to kiss her. He could not, of course. Not without muddling things more than they already were.

'Did your day go well?' he asked.

How she would occupy her time had been on his mind more than his ledgers. Hopefully she'd found an activity which would make her content. But the sense that he was letting her down would not go away...

'I was a complete failure, Andrew.' She dipped her forehead against his chest. A sigh and then a shudder took her. 'I failed.'

'Shall we have tea in the conservatory and discuss it?'

'Yes, please. I adore seeing the rain when I am not being soaked by it. I shall go upstairs and change, then meet you there.'

Andrew informed a maid that tea should be served in the conservatory, and then went there to wait. And to wonder what it was she had failed at. It was not like his wife to fail at anything...except that one thing which was not her fault but his.

She had looked too glum for the failure to have anything to do with being measured for a gown or trying on hats. This was something important to her.

Perhaps she had called on an old friend and been let down in some way. Or—and this gave his heart a turn—she might have gone to visit her first husband's grave and been prevented by the rain.

A surge of guilt squeezed his middle. If she had been turning to a dead man for the love that her liv-

ing husband refused her…well, then her living husband was not worth much.

Tea and Clara arrived in the conservatory at the
same time. His wife took the tray from the maid, gave
the young lady a smile, then sent her away.

She had changed into a gown of blue silk. And, as
modest as the garment was, all he could see was the
nightgown she'd worn to his room. It too had been
blue…but it had looked like mist, not silk.

No matter how he tried he was not able to stop seeing what had been beneath the mist.

It was fair to say he was haunted by the image.

'It is good to be home.' Clara sounded relieved when
she said so.

He slid out a chair and she sat down.

'With all the rain, I wonder how they are doing at
the estate.'

'As far as I know there are no leaks in the roof.
Would you like to tell me about what has gone wrong?'

'Not particularly, since I doubt you will approve.'

There it was, then. The place she had gone to *was*
the cemetery, and she had gone there to tell her former
husband how her current husband fell far short of him.

As true as that might be, he did not care to hear
her say so.

'I think you should tell me in case I can help,' he
said.

In case he was able to give her what Spencer had

given her: the proper love a man gave his wife. When only a week ago he had been certain he could not.

Now he did not know what he could or could not give her. Not for certain, at any rate, and he knew this was something a man needed be positive of.

'I do not wish for you to help,' she told him. 'I will do this on my own or not at all.'

On her own? What could she mean by that? How could she…? What was she speaking of if not what she had told him last week?

'I went to the factory to have a word with Mr Awful Smith.'

'You did what?'

She could not have!

'What sort of word? Clara, I will not have you going there without me.'

'What I spoke to him about is the fact that he has a large room which is not being used for anything and it ought to be donated for a Ragged School.'

'And he turned you down, I assume?'

'He said his way of helping children was to employ them, and that education would be wasted on them.'

Clearly upset in retelling what had happened, she leapt up, pushed away from the table and walked to the wall of windows that faced the garden.

He followed her.

Rain beat hard on the glass. She traced the path of

one raindrop with her fingertip as it zigzagged down the glass.

He placed his hands on her shoulders, gave them a gentle squeeze to offer comfort and support. At first she stiffened under his touch, then with apparent effort, she relaxed.

'I am not finished with Mr Smith,' she said. 'If he will not give the room for a school, I will demand a nursery for his employees to bring their children.'

'He will refuse you again, Clara. And I do not wish to see you distressed.'

'I will not be. I shall get what I want one way or another. If he will not give the room as a nursery, I will demand he establishes a clinic. If he refuses a clinic, I shall demand a shop, so the ladies can more easily clothe their families.'

'He will tell you no again and again. You cannot make him bend to your wishes.'

'I must find a way, Andrew.'

She turned about and looked up at him, the determination in her eyes clear.

'I need to be useful.'

'You are the most useful person I know.'

'Useful? Tell me, if you can, exactly who am I useful to?'

'To your family. They could not do without you.'

'Everything I used to do for them someone else now does. You are the one to have provided all they need.'

'*I* need you.'

She huffed out an offended little laugh. 'In what way, I wonder.'

He had it on his tongue to say in the same way all men needed their wives, but that was not true and she would surely point it out.

'To be a hostess?' she asked. 'I will point out that we do not entertain. And even if we did, fawning over society folk is hardly a worthy life endeavour.'

She'd used to think so—he was certain she had. He had seen the joy she'd taken in entertaining in the life she'd had before. Surely four years had not made such a difference.

'I remember that you looked fulfilled when you entertained before Spencer died.'

She turned back to the window. The wind blew rain every which way over the garden.

'I was. Of course. Only you misunderstand the reason for my fulfilment.'

'Clara, I...' His words trailed away, because he had no idea how to respond.

'Do not worry yourself about it. I did agree to marriage as we have it. Do not think I am complaining. You have done everything for us that you promised to do.'

'But I fear—' He feared it was not enough. But his confession died before he could see it through.

'No need to fear anything, my friend. I am grateful to you.'

He wondered if she had ever called her beloved Spencer her 'friend'. Or told him that she was grateful.

But grateful…? He would be satisfied with that. There were worse ways to feel about one's spouse than grateful.

An old memory came to him, popping out of his mind as if to argue against his last thought. One night when he was young… Christmas Eve it had been… he had crept quietly down the stairs to discover his mother sitting on his father's lap. They had been laughing quietly and kissing. Over and over again. Laughing and kissing.

When he had tiptoed back upstairs he'd felt grand about what he'd seen.

Years had gone by and he had never asked his mother the one thing he ought to have asked. Had loving his father been worth the price she had paid in grief?

He had always assumed it had not. Now, he wondered what her answer would have been.

But Clara was grateful to him…that would do.

Or he thought so until, looking into her eyes so full of gratitude, he recalled what her eyes had looked like when she'd looked at her first husband. He was taken aback for an instant.

'I wonder if it is enough,' he murmured.

'What is enough?'

'Gratitude...friendship...'

She patted his cheek, gave him a smile. 'We will make it enough.'

And all of a sudden he was the one who was not certain it could be.

Clara decided it was a good afternoon to take a walk. Warm and clear, it felt as if one might reach up and touch a cloud.

Besides, she had nothing else to do. Two weeks had gone by since she had failed at procuring a room for the Ragged School, and still she had found nothing worthy to occupy her hours. Unless one counted refraining from annoying the staff by joining them in their chores.

Funny how in her past life having nothing worthy to occupy her time had not troubled her. Making her husband shine in society was every well-bred lady's dream.

The difference between now and then was that life had changed her...taught her what made for a strong character.

Three days from now they were returning to London. Perhaps she would succeed in getting the miserly Mr Smith to provide a nursery for the children of his employees. She would volunteer her husband to find staff. All Smith would need to do was provide the space and pay them. Between now and then she would practise her speech, to be sure she did not leave out a single persuasive word which might sway him.

While they in London, she and Andrew would visit one more school. Afterwards, they would make a decision over George's education.

Since she was already out for a walk, Clara decided to go to the barn. She knew Annabeth's nurse had taken her to visit the lambs.

Spotting Georgie in one of the paddocks, she stopped to watch him. He dashed about, waving his arms and encouraging a pair of colts to run after him. It was quite clear that her son would rather become a stable master than a gentleman.

Having been denied the pleasures of fresh air and acres of green to romp in for so long, he was enjoying every second of it now. Perhaps they were making a mistake about sending him to a school in London. He might be better off at a local school, or with a tutor at home.

Going inside, she did not find her daughter in the barn, but she did find her sister. Lilly and a young stable hand were sitting on a bench beside the lamb pen.

With spring inching closer to summer, there were not as many lambs now. Most of them had been moved to the pasture along with their mothers. Not that the two young people seemed care. Their attention was only for one another.

How wonderful to be their age, with nothing more pressing to do than to laugh and chat. And to be holding hands while they did so.

Well, this was a surprise. Lilly's heart might yet be snatched away from the proper gentlemen who were vying for it…

Not wishing to disturb them, Clara backed quietly out of the stable. Perhaps Lilly had listened with at least one ear when Clara had advised her that love was better than a position in society. That happiness was more fulfilling than wealth.

Backing out through the big doors, she grinned, covering her mouth against a giggle. She stepped smack against something big and solid. Something male.

Not just any male.

Her male—whether he chose to accept all that went with it or not.

Turning in his arms, she looked up at him. Funny how he did not drop his arms from around her as she assumed he would.

Sunlight glinted on his hair, tempting her to touch it

and see if it felt as warm as it looked. He had an odd expression in his eyes which captured her attention more than the sun glinting in his hair did.

Yes, indeed, odd and intriguing.

And it was not her imagination that his gaze had settled intently on her lips. The way he looked at them made them feel warm…twitchy.

Since she must do something with them, or else go up on her toes and use them to kiss him, she said, 'What have you been up to this morning?'

'Ignoring what I ought to be doing in order to speak with my mother.'

'That must have been after Lilly and I had finished reading with her.'

'I cannot begin to thank you for spending time with her. It means the world to her…and to me.'

'Surely there is no need to thank me, Andrew. The time I spend with her is as precious to me as it is to her. I have spent so much time being a mother I had nearly forgot how good it feels to be a daughter.'

He cupped her chin, traced his thumb over her cheeks, shifting his gaze from her lips to her eyes.

'And to be a wife? Have you forgotten what that is as well?'

'I was a wife when you last saw me this morning, Andrew.' She understood what he was getting at but could not imagine why. Better to lead that thought down a different path. 'I have not forgotten since then.'

'No.' He dropped his hands from her, took a step back. 'I do not suppose you have.'

They stood for a while without speaking. No doubt each of them was trying to guess what was on the other's mind.

'I have been thinking,' she said at last, since one of them needed to say something and he seemed at a loss. 'I believe George should attend school nearer home.'

'I was going to say the same,' said Andrew. 'This is where he seems to be happy. And, given all he has been through, I believe it is best for him to be near you.'

'And the horses,' she said, gazing out at the paddock and seeing her boy with his arms about the neck of a colt. 'I am glad we agree.'

'Good—it is settled.'

Not everything was, though.

'Andrew...in case you are wondering if I am satisfied being your wife, and I think you might be, please be at rest about it. I could not be any happier than I am now. To see my Georgie playing with the horses rather than getting into scuffles at school and running away to work in a factory...that is all the happiness I need.'

They walked over the hill, ambling pleasantly towards the pond.

Clara rolled her shoulders. The sunshine felt good... rather like a caress.

'I have to say I am relieved that you are satisfied,'

Andrew said, going back to their conversation of a few moments ago. 'Don't you agree, though, that there are different degrees of satisfaction, according to the reasons for it? For instance, looking at lambs is more satisfying than looking at insects.'

'That is an odd comparison—but, yes, lambs are more pleasant than insects.'

'What I am getting at is this… The last time we were in London, and you had gone out for the morning, I thought you had been to visit your husband's grave. To tell him that…'

All at once he shook his head, sat down in the grass. He reached up a hand to bring her down beside him. Once she'd settled next to him he did not let go of her fingers but brought them to his chest and covered them with both of his hands.

'To tell him,' he continued, 'that I was falling far short of the husband he had been. I imagined him looking over my shoulder and condemning me.'

'First of all, Andrew Benton, I did not do that and nor would I. And in the future, when you refer to my husband, please keep in mind that you are he and I have no other.'

'I was in an odd mood when I imagined that.'

'What had you ingested to make you entertain such nonsense? Really, Andrew, as a husband you do not fall short of anyone. What I had with Spencer I had with Spencer, and it is gone. What I have with you is a thing apart. It is here…it is now. And, at the risk of making a muddle of everything, I will tell you the truth. I love you as much as I loved him.'

Oh, dear, she should probably not have blurted that out. 'Muddle' would not describe the mess she had made now. It would probably be worse than when she'd sneaked into his chamber.

She snatched back her hand and stood up.

What was done was done.

'Well, then, I have said what I have said…and now you know.'

With that, she lifted her skirts, ran back up the hill and down the other side. Reaching the garden, she paused for a moment to catch her breath.

When her ribs had stopped aching, she dashed though the house and into her chamber, where she closed the door.

Here she would remain until she had come to terms with the fact that, after what she said, her husband probably wanted nothing more to do with her.

And that was likely to be for the rest of her life.

Clara had not gone down for dinner, but pleaded a headache. One which would last until she had gathered the courage to live with the damage her loose tongue had caused.

But it was lonely up here by herself—especially

since she could not escape into a lovely, forgetful sleep.

She was standing by the window, watching Thor on his nightly outing, when she heard a light knocking on her door.

Please let it not be word that one of the children was ill. Annabeth had seemed so much better lately.

She yanked the door open, her heart creeping up her throat. Because what else could it be?

Oh, it could be Andrew.

Drat.

'I need your help with something, Clara. If you do not mind?'

'Let me get dressed first.'

She was rather certain he did not want the kind of help her nightgown might suggest.

Closing the door, she dressed, lickety-split. She could not imagine what he needed her for at this time of night.

His back was towards the door when she opened it. He spun about.

'I know it is late, but thank you, Clara.'

'Where are we going? What am I to help you with?'

'The staff's pay. Payroll is due tomorrow and I have been preoccupied most of the day. My accountant and I usually see to it together since I feel it is important that I have a hand in everything, but he is on a brief holiday. I have only just got to the bookwork.'

'Oh, Andrew! Thank you so much!'

'Thank me? It is I who am in your debt for coming down from your rest to help me. People do rely on getting paid on time.'

'I was not resting,' she said, going down the stairs beside him.

Moments ago she had expected her life to be full of woe. With a simple knock on the door it was suddenly a dream come true. For the next hour or so at least...

She prayed that his attitude would not be resentful while they worked side by side. Thus far it did not seem so.

She really should not have betrayed his trust by falling in love with him, but what was done was done.

At least he had called upon her when he'd needed help, so perhaps he was not as angry as she imagined.

Or was he simply desperate?

But whatever his mood was towards her, here she was.

It was not usual for a person to rejoice over being called from her bed to go over accounts. She did, however, feel a bit happy-go-lucky, skippy-skippy, going down the stairs.

Had she not glanced back at Andrew she would not have caught her toe in her gown and nearly stumbled.

He caught her elbow, yanked her to him.

To her amazement he was smiling at her!

She placed her hand on his chest. His heart thumped against her fingertips so forcefully that she felt it more strongly than she did her own.

Oh, indeed...happy-go-lucky, skippy-skippy.

'May I assume that since you are smiling you have forgiven me, Andrew?'

'For telling the truth about how you feel?'

He let go of her elbow, slipped his arm about her waist, then eased her down the last step. She did not need help... It was only, after all those months of life being hard, she did not mind being eased.

And simply being in Andrew's presence was akin to ease. At least it was now, since he was smiling. Earlier, though, when alone in her chamber and believing he hated her, she had been in misery.

'Yes, for that. I know it is not what you wish.'

'If we are speaking the truth, then I must tell you that I do not know what I wish.'

'You wish for the staff to be paid,' she pointed out.

They could go round and round about who felt what and then she would miss her chance to help with the pay ledgers.

'Shall we get to it, then?'

She took a pair of steps towards the office, but he caught her elbow, drew her back. Not to steady her this time but to throw her off balance. Because the 'it' he was getting to was kissing her...deep, long and hard.

This was the embrace of a man who wanted a woman and meant to have her. Of all the wicked, awful, wonderful and unbelievable timing...

She leaned into his kiss, wanting all of him.

And at the same she pressed him away with the palms of her hands.

Two dreams coming to pass at once. She could not have them both.

When she finally did push away, it was to breathe. And to ask, 'Why did you do that?'

'I told you. I no longer know what I want.'

Did he not? She knew what he was telling her and she knew what she was seeing in his eyes. He wanted to bed her...now...while the ledgers were waiting on his desk.

'This was a test, then? An experiment to see which way your sentiment would lean?'

'Honestly, I do not know. I wanted to kiss you. My motivation went no deeper.'

'We should go to the office,' she suggested...insisted.

Mercy! Whatever they were going to do, it could not be done in the corridor.

Chapter Nine

Clara appeared to be giving all her attention to what was written in the ledger.

His attention rested on her.

Numbers and names blurred in his vision.

If the payroll had not been needed first thing in the morning, those ledgers would not have been what was open on the desk.

It would have been his heart. He would have opened his soul and invited his wife in.

When he'd admitted to her an hour ago that he did not know what he wanted, it had been a lie. Or at best a hesitation.

What had changed him was his time with his mother. At the risk of opening old wounds, he had gone to her earlier in the day. He'd needed to know how, having been crushed at losing his father, she had then allowed herself to fall in love again.

He had not pointed out what a mistake it had been

to choose Parker Holmes, but the man's character was not the point. The point was, after nearly dying of a broken heart, why had she thought it acceptable to love again.

'For one thing,' she had said, 'I did not know that my dear Parker would also die. Really, my boy, I had no reason to believe we would not grow old and fat together.' She'd laughed after she'd said it, patting her middle. 'I have managed that last bit all on my own.'

'But you must have regretted marrying him after he died,' he'd said. 'You were depressed for a long time.'

'I hope you did not think so, Andrew. I regret that he died, not that I loved him.'

'That is what Clara says about her late husband.'

'She would, of course. What a wonderful woman she is. I hope you count your blessings every day that she agreed to marry you.'

'But, Mother, what if I allow myself to fall in love with her and then I lose her the way you did my father?'

'First of all, there is no allowing about it. You love her or you do not. As for losing her—you will. Either it will be at the end of her life or yours. Or it will be now, by spurning her love.'

'Did she tell you I was doing that?'

'Naturally not. But I have both eyes and experience.' She had patted his cheek. 'I love you, Andrew. Do not be a fool.'

And that had been it. She'd picked up her embroidery and begun to stitch, leaving him to decide between being a fool or a man who admitted he was in love.

'Clara,' he said. 'Do you wish to know why I did not get this work finished earlier?'

She glanced up from the page she had been concentrating intently upon, a pen poised between her thumb and finger. 'We are not finished now.'

He plucked the pen from her hand, set it aside. Rising from his side of the desk, he crossed to hers. There was another chair, so he pulled it close, placing them knee to knee.

'We are nearly. It will not hurt to pause for a moment.'

He took her hands, tried to rub a smudge of ink from her palm with his thumb.

'I like having it there,' she said.

'The ink or my thumb?'

'Both. But tell me why you did not take care of this earlier. It is not like you to put things off.'

'I mentioned that I'd spent some time with my mother?'

'Yes, you did.'

She arched a brow at him, clearly urging him to get

to the point. A thing he was anxious to do. But in a well-considered manner—with his thoughts in proper order. The last thing he wished was to stumble all over his words and confuse the issue.

'We discussed my father and why she chose to re-marry even after what she had suffered in losing him. I never understood it.'

'I see.' Her eyes and her voice were soft. 'And do you understand it now?'

'Better than I did. Although it would be easier to understand if she had married someone else. Then one could say that phrase about a door closing only to reveal an open door behind it...or all's well that ends well...or it was fate... But my mother had two closed doors...'

'Andrew, you are rambling.'

'I am putting my thoughts in order.'

'It does not seem to be working.'

Her lips were lifted in a beguiling smile. Secrets, and promises lurked in the pretty turn of her lips.

'It will all make sense in the end, I promise.'

'What do you promise, Andrew?'

'To give you a logical progression of—'

This profession of love was going to be as dry as crumbs, he thought. Dogs under the table would not eat them.

Standing suddenly, he yanked her up with him. Her

eyes grew round. Not startled, but curious. He lifted her under the arms and set her on top of the desk.

'I do know what I want. I want you.'

Now. He wanted her now.

He pressed her shoulders back. In the same movement she clasped his lapels and drew him down until they lay on the desktop, gleaming in the lamplight.

'I love you, Wife. And I will have you.'

'Right here on the ledgers?'

'You wanted to have a hand in them,' he said, against the soft skin under her ear.

'A hand, is it, Husband? It's more than that I shall be getting, I think.'

He laughed, deep in his throat. It was more a rumble coming up from his soul, which had been tamped down for far too long. And with a kiss that went to for ever and back, he made his intention known.

'It's a bold one you are, Andrew Benton...taking me on your desktop. But please do move aside the ink.'

'I like being bold,' he admitted, pausing to stopper the ink bottle and slide it to the far corner of the huge, shiny desk.

It was so shiny that he could see his grin reflected on the surface as he slid into position to fully make Clara his wife.

'I like it, too. Carry on, Andrew.'

* * *

When morning came Clara was no longer in the office but in Andrew's bedchamber, spooned into the curve of his big warm body. Rain slammed against the house in sheets. Lightning crackled in the sky and thunder hammered the hills.

She giggled as a thought came to her.

'What is it, love?'

'It's only that I have finally had a better night than Thor.'

Andrew went up on one elbow, gazed down at her. 'Thor?'

'Your friend the bull.'

'I promise you, Clara, a bull's amorous intentions do not resemble my devotion to you. Any cow will suit him just fine. You are the only heifer who will catch my eye again.'

'Oh, moo…'

How good it felt to indulge in such intimate silliness. She likened it to a love song only the two of them could sing.

He lifted the hank of hair that crossed her throat and spread it on the pillow with his long fingers. How delightfully carnal it was to catch the scent of her own skin on them.

Wedded bliss—that was what this was. Unexpected,

certainly, but at the same time hadn't she sensed this was where they were heading all along?

For a while last night she had been so happy, being allowed to add numbers and calculate wages. She hadn't thought she could want anything more. And then everything had changed. Andrew had put the desk to use in a better way. An intimate way.

Oh, mercy, she would always appreciate a good, solid desk...

'I never expected to have this, Clara.'

'I know. Are you frightened?'

He kissed her, so lightly and so sweetly. It was as powerful in its way as a bold, passionate kiss. It spoke of the everyday...the easy way they had between them.

'Terrified, if you want to know the truth,' he said.

'Don't worry. It's all a part of it. Joy and fear... No one can know what will happen.'

'I know about joy. It is right here in my bed, under my hands.'

'What do you say we make a bargain between us, Andrew?'

She patted his fingers, which seemed for all the world as if they were counting her ribs, from her waist to the ticklish spot between her shoulder blades.

'If it is never to get out of bed, then yes.'

She laughed. 'What a fine, lusty man I have married. But as to our agreement—let us make a pact that we will not fear what we cannot control. Let us make all our moments joyful. And do our best not to worry.'

'Agreed.' Finished with counting her ribs, he kissed away her sigh. 'Are you ready to indulge in more joy?' he asked.

'You know very well I am. But you are aware that we did not quite finish the payroll last night?'

'If I give everyone the day off I will not need to pay them until tomorrow.'

'That is not the rule! Besides, they have already begun working.'

'Very well. Indulge me a little longer and then we will go downstairs and set things right in the office.'

'Will Joseph return from holiday today? We did leave a little disorder behind.'

'He will only come if the rain lets up.'

'I hope it rains for ever, then. I adored helping you with the bookkeeping. Besides, it is something I ought to know for the good of our family.'

'Clara Benton, are you going back on our agreement already? You seem to be suggesting that something grim will happen.'

'Being prepared is not grim. However, being *un*-prepared is as foolish as can be.'

'I cannot put Joseph Billings out of his position.' He kissed her nose, smiled. 'But I would like it if you sat beside me while I work sometimes.'

'Truly? I should do it all the time if you'd let me.'

'But won't you be too busy for that? Convincing Smith to add a nursery to his factory will not be easy. Not to mention you will soon be busy with a certain small person who will fill your time.'

'Baby Andrew?' During the night the thought of having another child had crossed her mind a couple of times. How could it not, given the earnestness Andrew put into the task of its conception?

'Or Baby Clara. I wonder if we have time to apply ourselves to that goal one more time…'

'I do not suppose the staff will be spending their pay before noon anyway,' she said.

So for two more hours Mr Benton gave himself over to the endeavour, greatly aided by Mrs Benton.

As far as Andrew was concerned the world was right. Everything was as it should be.

How many years had he feared the very happiness he now could not live without?

But then, it was not the happiness he had feared, but losing it once he had it.

His mother was right, though, and so was his wife. Hadn't it been said that it was better to have loved and lost than never to have loved at all? Someone had said it… Although in that moment he did not recall who that fount of wisdom was.

It did not matter. Whoever had said it was correct.

Had he stupidly clung to his old way of thinking he would not now be free to stop in the wide corridor leading to the dining room, with the scent of food wafting out, to give his bride a long and lingering kiss.

A long and lingering kiss for every step.

At this rate they would miss lunch and only arrive at the table in time for dinner. Or not at all if they went back upstairs, as he had a strong urge to suggest.

Clara slid out of his embrace, gave him a look. 'Andrew Benton, you must eat if you wish to have enough strength—'

In the instant his mother bustled around the corner from the small parlour, smiling and clapping her hands.

'To finish the payroll, you mean?' he declared, so that Clara would not be embarrassed by what she might have said had Mother not suddenly appeared.

'The most wonderful thing has happened!' His mother glanced back over her shoulder and then at him and Clara. 'I can scarcely bear it!'

He might have known she would guess and be thrilled. It would only take her one look at his and Clara's smiles for it to be obvious.

'You will never guess!' Mother waited, as if taking joy in the added suspense. 'Your brother has come home!'

Clara went stiff under his arm. She covered a gasp

with her hand, but a fine tremor rippled through her shoulders.

Miles rounded the corner from the parlour a half-second later.

'No need to bother with the payroll,' he said, his voice as smooth as an adder's tongue. 'I have already—'

The sight of Clara holding on to his elbow had clearly stunned Miles for a moment. His grin fell so hard and so flat it was a wonder his face did not crack.

Because his mother had her back to him, she did not see her youngest son's reaction. And Miles was quick. By the time Mother turned to beam at him the smile was back.

'I have taken care of the payroll,' he went on, as smoothly as if he had not been shocked to see one of the women he swindled there in his brother's house. 'It is good to see you, Brother.'

Miles came forward as if to embrace him.

Clara took a step sideways, her frown a gathering storm.

'And Mrs Albright,' Miles went on, as if he did not notice the lightning crackling in her eyes. 'It is a pleasure to see you again. What a surprise.'

'Oh, indeed. A great surprise for us all,' she said, giving Miles a look down her nose which Andrew thought was far less severe than his brother deserved.

Clara would be within her rights to chastise Miles, to rip him up one way and down the other. He deserved to be exposed and escorted off the property.

'Oh, Miles, my dear. Having been away, you will not have heard.' Mother went to Clara, hugged her close. 'Clara Albright is now Clara Benton. You finally have a sister!'

The world went still…silent. Dread buzzed in Andrew's ears and made them throb in tempo with his heart. He could not ask Clara to hide the truth of what Miles had done to her. It would be unfair. The time had come for his brother to be exposed for what he had done.

But it sliced his soul that his mother would pay a higher price for it than Miles. It was too harsh. He was not sure she would be able to bear it.

'Truly?' Seeming to be recovered from the shock, Miles was at his charming best. 'I cannot tell you how pleased I am to hear the news. Welcome, Sister.'

Miles extended his hand.

Andrew took a step, placed himself between Clara and the man who had ruined her. She should not have to go through this.

But before he could fully face off with his brother, Clara had extended her hand to Miles.

'Thank you, Miles. It is good to see you again. I trust you had a successful trip?'

Andrew was certain to his bones that he had never loved anyone more than he did Clara Benton. Because of her compassion he was not carrying his mother to her chamber, confused and weeping.

'Isn't it the most wonderful thing in the world for a family to be together?' his mother was saying. 'No mother was ever more blessed than I am.'

This was the truth—more than his mother had any way of knowing.

'Meet me in my office, Miles,' he said. 'We have matters to catch up with.'

Then, with an arm around Clara's waist, Andrew led her to the hall and then out through the front door.

He crushed her to him. Bent his head to her shoulder. He was an inch from a great sob shaking loose a flood of tears.

'Clara, my love, you do not have to do this. I will send him away.'

'Nonsense. I told you I would not do anything to hurt your mother. Miles might very well be the worst person I know, but your mother is among the most loving.'

Rain poured off the portico, muffling their conversation. Clara lifted her face, peered hard into his eyes, which he knew must look as damp as the stones they stood on.

'Andrew, you know this… Love is stronger than

hate. And that is how we will get through this mess. But now I must find the children and warn them. They will need a reminder of how much they love their new grandmother. I think, living here, they have almost forgotten the damage Miles did to us. I do not want them to blurt out anything hateful when they remember.'

'Very well. I will find you after I have had a few words with my brother,' he said. 'But you will not mind if I hit him, just once?'

She arched her brows, lifted herself on her toes and kissed him. 'Oh, I am counting on it, Husband. Once for you and once for me.'

Andrew passed his mother in the corridor on the way to his office, where he meant to confront his brother. Her face was so pink with pleasure that he could not help but stop and kiss her cheek.

'I love you, Mother,' he said, reminding himself of what Clara had impressed upon him by word and by example.

Love was stronger than hate. He would need to keep that in mind in order to deal with Miles.

Going further down the corridor, he went inside his office to find his brother lounging in the desk chair, ankles crossed and the heel of his shoe negligently on the desktop.

The very desktop on which Andrew's life had changed last night. It was as if Clara had picked up a pen and rewritten his life's story—except, of course, she had not used a pen...

'Get up, Miles,' he snapped.

With a great resigned sigh his brother stood, walked around to the other side of the desk. As Miles brushed by him Andrew drew back his hand, curled it into a light fist and hit him in the chin.

'What kind of way is that to welcome your long-lost brother?' Miles complained, rubbing his jaw even though Andrew had not hit him hard enough to injure him, only to make a point.

The last thing he wished was to explain to his mother how her darling child had got bruised.

'The most appropriate way I can think of,' Andrew said. Then he hit him again.

'What the blazes, Andrew?'

'That one was for Clara. She would like to do it herself, you understand, but she has left the pleasure to me.'

'Pleasure? Are you insane? I am an innocent man. I never cheated that old widow. Why do you think they let me out early?'

Andrew sat down in his chair. Opened the top drawer. Shuffled though the papers he had carefully stored there.

'Everyone could see the old lady was addled,' Miles

went on. 'The way I look at it, she and that son of hers owe me for the time I spent locked away.'

Finding what he was looking for, Andrew slapped it down on the desk. 'Do you recognise this, Miles?'

His brother sat in the chair across the desk, arrogantly slouched with his leg crossed over his knee. He shrugged.

'Shall I read it to you?'

'Oh, I have seen it. Clara Albright…oh, I beg your pardon, Clara *Benton*…wrote it herself, you know. All those lies… My guess is that she meant to sue me. Get some money after she'd spent all she had. Some women are greedy that way. What I cannot understand is why you married her.'

Red-hot rage pumped through Andrew's veins. Since nothing would be gained by giving in to it, he took a moment to breathe and collect his temper. The two punches he had already delivered would have to be enough.

'I married her because you left her and her family destitute, all but starving, in a dangerous part of town. Did you even give her a thought, Miles?'

'Why would I? I told you she made all that up.'

'I can't work out who you are trying to lie to. All three of us know the truth. The only one who does not is our mother.'

At last Miles had the good grace to appear ashamed.

'I wish you had not come home,' Andrew continued. 'It will be a strain on everyone. Even the children know who you are and what you did to them. But since you are here this is how it will be. Mother must be protected at all costs. It would break her beyond hope to know what you really are.'

'And you think your wife is not going to give me away? That is naïve of you. But you never were much good with women.'

'Don't you wonder why she did not expose you when she first saw you?'

Miles shrugged, kept silent.

'She had every right to.' Andrew was clinging to the very edge of his patience.

'What if she changes her mind?'

'She will not—and shall I tell you why?'

'I assume you are going to, no matter how I feel about it.'

'She simply loves Mother more than she detests you.'

'How noble. Sounds like something your minister father would have said.'

'You never knew my father and you cannot know what he would say.'

'Mother had a hundred stories about how decent he was even after she was married to my father.'

'She had a hundred stories about how charming *your* father was too.'

Now would be the time to point out that he had also

been a scoundrel, but there was no point since Miles already knew.

'I wonder how long it will be until your wife convinces you to send me away from my own home,' said Miles. 'A week…a month?'

'I will be watching you, Miles. What I decide depends upon you. For Mother's sake, my family will treat you civilly. I expect the same behaviour of you.'

'And what about you? How will *you* treat me? As I see it, your exaggerated sense of duty has made you feel you need to make up for my…my *lapse*, shall we call it? It forced you to marry the widow. I can only assume you blame me.'

'What you did to my wife and my children was not a "lapse". It was intentional…despicable. I hope that somewhere in your soul you recognise that. That you repent of it.'

'Ah, there again—I hear your father preaching through you. No, Andrew, I do not blame myself for your fate. What you have done is on you, not me.'

'You greatly mistake my relationship with my wife.'

'Do I? You never had any intention of taking a wife before.'

'If you are here long enough you will see for yourself.'

'So, those are the rules? Be a good boy…polite as the dickens.' He shrugged. 'Very well. No one will be able to tell me from a saint.'

'One more thing. You will have no hand whatsoever in keeping the family books.'

'I am the one who has had the training for it—but as you wish.'

Miles stood, his mouth pressed into a thin, tight line. No doubt his homecoming was not quite as he'd expected it to be. With Clara here, he would not be able to charm everyone into believing him innocent.

'Shall we go to lunch and discover just how much your new family loves our mother?'

With no outward hesitation Clara smiled when Miles pulled out a chair for her. It was among the hardest things she had ever done, but she sat beside him.

Equally difficult was maintaining that smile and making it appear as if she was delighted to see him safely home from his 'trip to the continent'.

Oh, how false the pair of them were...putting on a show of family fidelity.

It was only seeing her mother-in-law lean close to her youngest son, smiling and hanging upon every lie he told her about his great adventure in France, that made it possible to keep her composure.

Love is stronger than hate, she reminded herself... again. She did believe that. Only just now her resolve to follow that principle was stretched as thin as a thread of silk. But, like silk, it was durable.

'It sounds like such a grand adventure, Miles,' she

said. 'It is no wonder you did not have time to write home.'

'But I wrote often!' He gave his mother a glance which for all the world indicated surprise. 'You did not get my letters?'

'No, my boy. But, oh, how I wish I had. It would have put my mind at rest.'

'Oh, then you must not have received my gift either?' Miles said.

'You sent me a gift?' Mrs Benton leaned sideways and kissed her son's low-down, lying face. 'You are the most thoughtful son...and the very image of your father.'

From all Clara had heard, he was his father all over.

'I am the image of *my* father, too,' Georgie declared.

'Indeed you are.' Clara wished she could lean across the wide table and kiss him. 'And I am grateful every day for it.'

'I remember your father being the very best of men, George,' said Andrew, ruffling George's hair with his large palm.

And George's second father was as wonderful as the one he had been born to. Clara had good reason to know it.

Her love for her husband grew deeper by the second. He was her hero in every way she could imagine.

She fancied—quite vividly, in fact—that Andrew's father was gazing down upon him in pride. She knew she would do her best to make him proud of his new daughter-in-law. Not that it would be an easy thing where Miles was concerned. Turning the other cheek would be a great challenge…

'I suppose the post is not always what it should be.' Clara directed her comment towards her mother-in-law. If she'd looked at Miles when she spoke it would have come off as sarcastic. 'A parcel might easily get lost.'

Everyone at the table knew there had been no letters, no gifts.

For the past two years Clara had indulged in fantasies of retribution on Miles Holmes if she ever met him again. Not a single time had she expected to cover his lies.

Once again, she reminded herself that she was not doing it for the conniving Miles, but for his vulnerable mother.

'Isn't this a slice of Heaven, my dears?' Mrs Benton wrapped her arms about herself in a hug, and gave a happy wriggle. 'We are the luckiest people in the world. For so long it was only the three of us, and now there are four more.'

Standing, she walked in a circle around the table, stopping to kiss each person on the cheek.

Clara was the last person Mrs Benton came to. Cupping Clara's cheeks in her prettily aged hands, she declared, 'And very soon we will be more.'

Luckily, his mother would not see the face Miles made at that pronouncement. Clara caught it all too clearly. There and gone, covered quickly by a smile where before there had been a nasty smirk.

'I imagine you cannot wait to be an uncle, Miles,' Clara said, with a well-disguised smirk of her own.

She might have pointed out that he already was, with Annabeth and Georgie, but...

Oh, no! She would not give that man anything she did not have to.

'I shall wait with bated breath for the happy news.'

His mother was probably the only one of the adults not to catch the sarcasm in that statement.

'It will be the grandest day ever. We shall have a great party to celebrate. Or perhaps we should have one now, to celebrate Miles coming home from the Continent at long last. We shall invite all the neighbours and have a double celebration in honour of your marriage, Andrew.'

'I will give the matter some thought,' he answered.

Clara knew that the party would not happen. Too many people knew where Miles had been. Someone was bound to say something. Gossip would be heard. His mother must be protected. That was one matter they would all agree on.

All Clara wanted was to get through this day, put her children to bed and then put herself to bed in her husband's chamber, tucked into the curve of his warm chest and strong thighs. Only then would she exhale a sigh of relief.

She was not accustomed to holding her tongue. Oh, how many times within the past quarter-hour had she resisted the urge to poke Miles's hand with a fork? Or to pour hot cocoa into his lap and pretend it was an accident?

Hopefully lunch would be over soon. Because now the thought of hot cocoa had come into her mind it would not go away. The interesting thing was, Lilly was also looking at her drink in a curious way. And why not? They were sisters, and their thoughts tended to lean the same way.

Unlike the others, Lilly was not so young that she did not remember the damage Miles had done. Missing two years of society had been hard on her. Although now, after seeing Lilly with the young stableman, Clara wondered if her sister was seeing her future in a different light.

Hopefully she was.

Having lived in wealth and lived in poverty, Clara had learned one thing. Love mattered more.

Everyone sitting about the table chattered on while she wandered away in her thoughts.

If she were given a choice between going upstairs to a well-appointed chamber with every comfort a lady could wish for, but lying in her bed alone, or going back to the slum and sharing a bed with Andrew... Well, she would pick her husband every single time.

No amount of money could make her feel more secure than his arms around her did.

She was rather stunned to find that she felt almost half a teaspoon full of sorry for Miles. No matter how many people he'd bamboozled, he could not steal love. All his efforts earned him was to be despised and resented.

She became aware of everyone standing. Good, then. With lunch over they would not need to come together again until dinner. After that it would only be a short time until she and Andrew would find sanctuary in his chamber.

Tomorrow, she would have someone remove the door separating her chamber from his. There was no need for it any longer. The issues which had once kept them apart were gone. From now on it would simply be the two of them, free to love each other all day, all night...all their lives.

Summer was winding down. Andrew's pleasant hours of strolling over green hills in warm sunshine with Clara would soon cool.

'We need to do this as often we can before the weather turns,' Andrew said, whispering close to her ear.

No one was nearby, so there was no need to whisper. He only did it to breathe in the fresh, sunny scent of her hair.

'I look forward to the weather changing,' she said. 'We shall build a fire in the hearth and snuggle under a blanket in one chair.'

'Hmmm…' He nuzzled his nose into the soft ringlets near her temple. They tickled, making him grin. What a grand fool he had been to fight falling in love with this woman. 'I used to be sorry to see summer end. What you have just said has changed my mind. Are we to be dressed under the blanket? Please say we are not.'

'I'll say it again…it is a bold one that you are, Andrew Benton. Bold and with a creative mind. I will let you decide about the clothes. As for autumn… I promise you will love it.'

'You will need to teach me.'

'It might take practice.' She stopped walking and wrapped her arms around his middle. 'A great deal of practice to appreciate a season when you never have before.'

'I have always been a dedicated student,' he admitted, feeling his grin stretch wider across his face. 'I imagine kisses under a shared blanket will last longer than normal ones?'

'Indeed. Under the privacy of a blanket anything can happen.'

'I have a feeling autumn might become my favourite season.'

He hadn't felt that way in the past, but there seemed to be no limit to the good things he was learning since he'd met Clara. His wife was changing him in ways he never would have believed.

They strolled over the rise of the hill leading to the pond. He hoped to strip off his shoes and stockings, roll down Clara's too, and go for a wade in the water.

He could only guess where the undressing might lead…

But blast it. Nothing would be coming off.

His mother and Miles sat at the water's edge. Mother was laughing at something Miles had told her. No doubt he was inventing a grand tale of what had never happened in Paris.

Three weeks had passed since his brother had been released from prison and had had the audacity to come home as if nothing had happened. As if he had done no wrong.

Andrew watched Miles slip his arms across Mother's shoulders and gave her a quick hug. Their combined laughter drifted up the hillside.

So far he had not caught his brother in any wrongdoing…not any that was obvious. But that did not mean he would not be wary.

'It is becoming easier,' Clara said. 'Being around

him. Not as prickly. It is worth a great deal to see your mother this happy.'

In that instant, Miles and Mother spotted them, waved in greeting. If he did not know better he would imagine his brother was as honourable as a hymn in church.

'It is not only Mother's happiness which counts,' he said. 'Yours is every bit as important.'

Clara smiled, waved back.

'Are you looking for compliments for your thoughtfulness, husband? If so, I will give them.'

She whispered in his ear, describing last night and the ways he had been thoughtful and attentive in every way.

He could give a sizzling compliment as good he got. He took his turn to whisper in her ear. Then they laughed.

Hearing them, his mother glanced away from Miles, sent them another wave and an indulgent smile. Miles gave them a curious one.

'I wonder if I will ever come close to trusting him again,' he murmured as they turned about and walked back down the side of the hill they had just climbed and towards the barn.

'You are too clever for that, I think.'

'Am I? Perhaps not. Had I been all that clever in

the past I would have been aware that he was cheating you. I would have kept it from happening.'

'Andrew Benton, if I hear one more word of misplaced guilt come out of our mouth... Well, you do not wish to know what I will do.'

'I think I do wish to know.' He could not help but smile. Whatever she had in mind would be interesting.

'You will have to wait. I have not yet decided your fate. But you will be...'

'Delighted?'

'Lectured, I think.'

'In words?' He arched a brow.

She answered with a frown, its severity softened when one corner of her mouth tipped up. 'That is how it will begin.'

'Ah... Look, Wife. We have come to the barn. I am ready to be lectured.'

It was the lazy part of the afternoon. And this was the day for Bosing and the farm hands to go to the village for supplies.

The stable was dim, wonderfully deserted.

There would be privacy for whatever Clara had in mind after her lecture.

Coming inside, Andrew sat on the bench beside the lamb pen. It was empty at this time of year, with the lambs old enough to be at pasture.

'I am ready,' he announced with a grin.

'You think you are, Andrew Benton.' She stood, hands folded on her hips, and gave him that delightfully stern look down her nose. 'But I am serious in what I have to say.'

'I am serious in hearing it.'

'Here you are, then. I am good and done with hearing about how guilty you feel for something you did not do. How you somehow ought to have been aware of you brother's actions, as if you did not have anything else to occupy your attention.' She pointed her finger at him, righteous fire igniting the green flecks in her eyes. 'Should you begin to succumb to such illogical emotions you will keep them to yourself and not trouble me with them.'

'Very well,' he agreed.

She was correct. It did not fall to her to comfort his guilt over and over again.

She sat on his lap, softening her attitude, but he did not feel the lecture was finished.

'Don't you see, Andrew? If Miles had never done what he did everything would be different. We would not be the people we have become. The people we used to be would not have fallen in love. I would have continued my comfortable pursuits of entertaining and embroidering. You would have gone on to wed a convenient lady who did not require that you love her.'

He would have avoided marriage as best he could,

but what she said was right. His life might well have turned out as she described it.

'So, you are implying that had it not been for Miles robbing you I might have ended up a sad and miserable fool?'

'No, Andrew, I am not implying. I am stating it as fact. We had a road to travel to get to one another. We could not have come together in any other way than we did.'

'I would go through hell to get to you, Clara,' he said, suddenly serious.

'Well...' She kissed the tip of his nose. 'It is not as dire as all that. Still, I would not have chosen an easier path if it had not led to you in the end.'

She was correct. Going through what they had, had been the only way they could be together.

'I will never feel guilty for it again,' he vowed.

'And now that my lecture is finished, will you fetch a blanket and meet me on top of that pile of fresh straw?'

She stood, winked.

He fetched the blanket at a run.

Chapter Ten

'Clara, may I have a word?'

Everything in her wanted to refuse to speak with Miles. In the month he had been at home she had not had a private conversation with him. A situation which suited her well. However, it had become fairly easy being polite to him when Mrs Benton was present.

She could not think of what they might have to say to one another which would not ruin the fragile peace they had managed to create within the household.

'I need to speak with Cook about the menu,' she told him.

'May I walk with you, then?'

Since there was no way to prevent him from doing so, she shrugged, nodded. 'Very well, Miles. I imagine we do have things to settle between us.'

They walked away from the parlour and down the corridor towards the kitchen.

'I want to say that I have misjudged something and I wish to apologise for it.'

'Indeed. What is it?' This is not what she'd expected, but she was curious.

'When I got home and discovered you had married my brother, I believed he had married against his will. I see that I am mistaken. I apologise for thinking you had taken advantage of his absurdly strong sense of right and wrong.'

'Honour is never absurd—although I do not expect that you understand that. But be at peace where you brother is concerned. I love him. We are happy in our marriage.'

'I can see how he loves you. I admit to envying the two of you that.'

His smile seemed sincere. She had to remind herself that charm was a tool he wielded, a fine-honed weapon.

'Are we finished?' she asked, pausing beside the kitchen door.

'So anxious to be rid of my company, Clara? I remember a time when we were friendly. I was a regular visitor to your home.'

The home he had ruthlessly stolen from her. From his manner, it seemed as if he had forgotten about that small, life-shattering matter.

'Of course.' She glanced about, to be sure no one was within earshot. 'I imagine I made an easy target, inviting you in and trusting that you were seeing to my investments. But a veritable wolf at the door is what you were—not a friend at all.'

'I would plead that I made an honest mistake in mishandling your money. However, I cannot, since my brother discovered otherwise. I can only say that I regret what I did.'

'I cannot imagine why I should believe that.'

'Who would blame you, naturally? But this much is true: I love my mother. I have always struggled to make her proud of me. Andrew was the perfect one.'

'If you believe your mother loves you less than she does Andrew, that is on you. She has the biggest heart of anyone I have ever met. She thinks you and your father are the most wonderful men ever to have walked the earth. Do not try and use her to excuse your behaviour, Miles.'

'No…that is not my intention… Well, perhaps a bit. But the truth is, I do love my mother. I am grateful you have not exposed me to her. That is all I wanted to tell you.'

'I love your mother too—which is why I have no intention of revealing what you did.'

'I thank you for that.' He nodded and proceeded down the corridor, then said over his shoulder, 'I am happy it has worked out for you and Andrew.'

She was not certain he meant anything he'd said

except that he loved his mother. The rest could easily be bald-faced fibs.

Truth or lie—it made no difference to how she would behave towards him.

She simply cared for Mrs Benton more than she resented Miles.

London, Clara decided, while looking out through the carriage window at the people rushing along the pavements, past buildings set close together, was not as nice as the country estate—not even at its finest.

At its worst, the city was miserable and dangerous. A place she felt needed a great deal of improvement.

After rushing up the town house steps, the first thing she did was look for her husband.

She found him in his study. On a half-choked sob she threw herself at him…and then she let loose and wept.

'He refused you again?'

Clara nodded and sniffled against Andrew's waist-coat. 'Frederick Smith is the worst person I have ever met.'

Andrew's arms enfolded her. 'I will not forbid your visits, but really, my love, it is only breaking your heart every time he turns you down.'

'Forbid? Are you trying to cheer me up by making jokes, Andrew? Oh, but it makes me furious, thinking about how he refuses to spend one penny to make life better for his workers. And these are angry tears—not defeated ones.'

'I have never known you to be defeated by anything.'

'So far that black-hearted soul has refused the clinic, the school *and* the nursery.'

'You will win him over with the shop. It is a brilliant idea.'

'It worked well in the past. But I'll need to wait a while before I renew my attack.'

She loosened herself from Andrew's arms, feeling steadier now. She did not need his arms around her to feel grounded. Simply knowing he was nearby made her secure.

'I will give him time to settle before presenting my demand for a shop.'

'You are home just in time for tea,' he said.

'Perfect. It is getting colder outside.'

'It is nearly autumn. Only another week. We should engage in that activity you told me about and sit before the fireplace tonight under a blanket. In the chair... do you remember?'

Oh, indeed. And just thinking about it chased away the chill and the angst she had come home with.

Hours later, Andrew had his wife under a fluffy blanket, both of them bare as hatchlings.

'This feels like a nest,' he told her.

'I wish we never had to leave it,' she said, snuggling her head against his shoulder.

But as wonderful as never leaving it would be, life called. And it was time he told her where it was soon to call him.

Going away on business had never troubled him in the past. He had always enjoyed going to Paris, meeting people and purchasing fabric to bring home and sell. It had been an adventure.

Lately, all the adventure he needed was under this blanket. And it was also in raising the children who had come to him by way of Spencer Albright.

Ah, well... If he intended to provide for them as a proper father he would need to be gone from time to time. Money did not earn itself.

'Clara, my love. I have something I must do.'

She began to move away from him, lifting the corner of the blanket. 'Don't be long about it. I do not wish to get cold and lonely.'

He wished she had not said 'cold and lonely', since that was what the very near future held. Cold days and lonely nights.

But there was no point in putting off what needed saying.

'What I mean is that I must go to Paris on business. I do it every year at this time.'

'When?' She sat up straight and the blanket fell away.

This separation was going to be harder than he'd

imagined. Having realised that a loving marriage was what he wanted, he did not want to be away from his wife for even a day.

'In two weeks. I will be gone no more than a week. After that I will not need to go again until early spring.'

She hugged him tight. He might even have heard his ribs creak.

'Until then I shall hold on to you very tight,' she said.

'I was counting on that, Mrs Benton.'

He drew the blanket back over them.

Andrew had been gone for a week. A long week which to Clara seemed more like a month.

She felt adrift. It was odd that after all the time she'd spent on her own, not even knowing who Andrew was, she should feel that way.

In those days she had not felt adrift. There had been a purpose to each day. Survival tended to ground a person in a way nothing else could.

Very likely the difference between then and now had to do with the fact that her time was no longer occupied with providing food and protection. At all times someone was nearby to provide those day-to-day things.

Lately her time had been about waiting, but Andrew was expected home tonight or tomorrow.

She was so excited about it that her stomach was on edge. Even the briefest glance at the cherry scones on the tea tray made her want to flee to her chamber. Excitement would do that, she supposed.

Blustery weather had kept almost everyone inside today. She, Mrs Benton and Lilly sat in the parlour, stitching roses on pillowcases. But Miles had gone to the village.

It was always a relief when he went away for periods of time. He had not acted unpleasantly towards her in Andrew's absence. And if he did not approve of her sitting with Joseph Billings while he worked on the accounts he did not say so. But who could know for certain what was going on inside his conniving soul?

There was one matter she was certain he was honest in. He did love his mother. It could not be denied that ever since he'd returned he had been attentive to her every need.

No son doted more upon his mother. It must he his one saving grace.

It probably also had to do with his mother being the only person who loved him unconditionally.

Being a mother, Clara understood that universal devotion.

Moments ticked by too slowly as she watched the

parlour clock in anticipation of seeing Andrew. She ought to have it taken down.

'If that wind blows any harder it will take the roof with it,' Mrs Benton said with a shiver. 'I wish Miles would come home. I would feel so much better with a man in the house.'

Clara was half tempted to point out that they would be better off without Miles as protector. But she must be getting used to having him about, because there had been a time when it would have taken all her resolve not to point out this fact. That it now took only half her effort was progress, she supposed.

'We have many dependable men on our staff. I am certain we have no reason to worry,' she said.

If the glass doors now rattling on their hinges broke open in the wind, the staff would be better at dealing with the situation than Miles would be. It would be no great loss if the storm kept Miles in the village overnight.

'Oh, my, but that wind is beastly,' Andrew's mother murmured, with a worried glance at the doors. 'I hate to think of my sweet boys out in it. I will not be at ease until I know they are home and safe.'

Only a moment later the front door opened. Miles's voice filtered in from the hall. His mother's heart would be put to rest over one of her sons.

If only Andrew's voice would filter in from the

hall. He could be a mile from home or still in Paris, for all she knew. If only there was a way to know where a person's loved ones were at all times. Some magical communication. That would eliminate a lot of concern.

Miles was speaking with the butler in low tones. Even from here she could hear the agitation in his voice. Perhaps it had to do with miserable road conditions.

He came into the parlour, his hair wet and hanging across his eyes, his breathing laboured and his eyes red. Something was dreadfully, horribly wrong.

Clara slowly stood, the needlework slipping off her lap. It hit the floor with a thump. Miles's heavy breathing was the only sound after that.

He looked at Mrs Benton, then turned his gaze to Clara.

'Andrew's ship is missing. The news came when I was at the inn. They say that the storm in the Channel was fierce. His ship never made port. There was another ship which reported seeing it in trouble. The authorities fear it is lost...'

He crossed the room, clasped Clara's hands and squeezed them. Next, he went to his mother and knelt before her.

'It is feared that all souls are lost.'

Mrs Benton gave a cry. Miles wrapped her in his

arms and glanced over his shoulder at Clara, his eyes swollen.

'I am so sorry to bring this news.'

'But no one saw the ship go down? Saw it with their own eyes?'

Gossip was not proof of anything.

He shook his head. 'But it must be presumed...'

No. She would not be a widow again. Not so soon. It was quite impossible. No...no and no. She would not accept this until she saw the ship's wreckage with her own eyes...unless she held her husband's body and wept over it.

'I presume nothing of the kind,' she said.

Mrs Benton sobbed, then gasped.

Miles, still on his knees, patted her back. 'Do not worry, Mother,' he whispered. 'I am here.'

Oh, indeed he was...and offering no hope whatsoever.

'Move aside, Miles. Give your mother space to breathe.'

Perhaps Clara sounded harsh, but hope was what was needed in that moment—not rumours reported as fact. Inn talk.

To tell his mother that her son had died without having absolute proof was unacceptable. Even Miles must know that. Given her emotional history, she might very well become despondent. If she was to make it through this what she needed was courage.

Miles did not appear to understand that. He swung his head to glare at her though his tears. 'It is unkind of you to offer hope when none exists,' he snapped, without moving from the spot.

Clara knelt down, hip to hip beside Miles. As near as they were, they were far distant in their opinions about what was needed in this moment.

'Dry your eyes, Mother.' Clara picked up the hand Miles did not have clutched to his heart. She kissed Mrs Benton's trembling fingers. 'Miles has heard a horrible thing. So far we have no reason to believe what he has heard is true. Until the authorities come and present us with proof, we should take it for what it is…only talk.'

'Perhaps you are right. Oh, my dear, I hope so.' Her mother-in-law took a deep, trembling breath. 'You aren't worried?'

'Oh, Mother, I am terrified. You know I am. We both know how this could crush us. But let us not allow it to until we know for certain that we must face tragedy.'

'Yes, of course. Our Andrew might come home, and then we will have wasted away for nothing.'

'We will all have great courage. And when Andrew returns he will be so proud of us for bearing up,' Lilly declared shakily.

'I want to make my son proud…'

'And I want to make my husband proud,' said Clara.

'I say we continue to stitch our roses.' Lilly lifted her needle, plunged a strand of red thread into the pillowcase. 'I believe we will dine with Andrew tomorrow…perhaps even tonight.'

'You ladies carry on.' Miles stood, his frown shifting between Clara and Lilly. 'I will be in Andrew's office, finding a way to see us through this crisis financially.'

He strode from the room, grief evident in the slump of his shoulders. The man might be unscrupulous, but he did care for the brother who had all but raised him.

Clara identified with his tears.

She felt them pressing at her heart, at her resolve not to fall to her knees and sob.

Perhaps the only thing keeping her from doing so was seeing Andrew's mother gazing up at her with watery eyes and a tremulous smile.

As it turned out, Andrew did not come home for dinner that night. Nor the next night, or the next.

The last thing Clara wished to do was get out of bed, to face what her life had become… An agony of waiting, fighting off grief with every breath. Still, the battle became harder with each day her husband did not return.

Convincing his mother that there was every reason to hope was nearly impossible. More and more she was beginning to think she was spinning some great lie to herself and everyone else.

But whatever the truth turned out to be, she knew she must get out of bed.

Her queasy stomach was becoming insistent. Perhaps once she was on her feet it would settle.

But standing, made it worse.

She made a dash for the washstand. Bent over at the waist as her stomach emptied.

Well, then…

She touched her middle, blinked at a rush of tears. 'Hello, Baby Benton. It is beyond wonderful to make your acquaintance. Your father will be so pleased to meet you when he comes home…'

She slipped down. Kneeling on the floor, she bent her head to her knees and sobbed.

For a few moments she would indulge. If she did not weep she might explode. Which she could not do. Her family depended upon her. This tender new baby especially.

It could not be that she was in the same situation she had been in four years ago. A pregnant widow, her funds being managed by Miles Holmes.

Yesterday afternoon Andrew's accountant had come to her, distraught at having been dismissed from his position. Knowing of Miles's past, Joseph Billings had good reason to worry.

Last night, when she'd confronted Miles about it,

he had informed her that she was no longer permitted in the office. Women, he insisted did not have the sort of brain to work with numbers. Then he'd smiled, told her she did not need to worry, that he had her financial wellbeing in hand.

She wondered if he had purposely used the very same words he had used before, assuring her that all would be well while he was robbing her of all she had.

Taking a long, trembling breath settled her stomach. A moment later she had her tears under control and rose from the floor.

She might be a widow—she had no control over that. What she would not be again was Miles Holmes's victim. Nor would anyone who belonged to her. Never again would her family be put out in the cold, dependent upon the charity of a fish vendor to survive.

This time she knew her enemy. This time she would fight him.

When her maid came in she asked to be dressed in her most cheerful gown, and for a happy bow to be added to her hairstyle and a red brooch fastened to her collar.

Reviewing her image in the mirror, she lifted her chin. A knight of old would not have been better equipped for battle.

Given that she was late going down, she knew the family would already be eating breakfast.

'Good morning, my loves,' she said, stopping to give each person a kiss. 'Good morning, Miles.'

No kiss for him—only a nod and a smile. It would not do to be overly friendly to him or he would suspect she was up to something.

Which she most definitely was.

'You seem well this morning, Clara.' Miles returned her smile.

Hmph…was his smile as false as hers? Whether it was or not, she refused to be fooled by it. Not again…not ever.

'Why would I not be? Each day that passes is one day closer to Andrew coming home.'

'But it's so muddy, Mama,' Annabeth pointed out. 'Papa will get stuck.'

'I do not want you to worry, Annabeth. There is not enough mud in the world to keep Papa from us.'

Miles stood. 'May I have a word with you, Sister?'

'Of course. But first I must eat. I am absolutely starving.' She chewed a bite of ham. She actually was hungry for once. 'Will you be in the office?'

'Yes—meet me there.'

She took her time eating, not wishing for Miles to guess that the office was exactly where she wished to be.

Several minutes later Annabeth's nurse came for her, and George ran off to play with the three kittens he had brought in from the stable yesterday.

'Clara, my dear… Do you really believe today will be the day our Andrew comes home?' asked her mother-in-law.

'It might be. I certainly hope it is.'

'I am trying not to lose hope. But I do not know how much longer I can go on…'

Clara picked up her plate of food, took it to Mrs Benton's side at the table. She slid her chair close. There was a time to keep a secret and a time to reveal one.

'There is a very good reason you must not give in to despair,' she said. She knew Andrew ought to be the first she told, but it was important for his mother to have the good news now. She was certain he would agree. 'May I share a secret with you, Mother? You will not tell anyone?'

'You may trust me with it, daughter.'

'This is news you will want to share, but it is best if it is just between us for now.'

'Does it have to do with my son? Have you had word of Andrew?'

'I have not had word of him, but this has a great deal to do with him. You are the very first to know… I am expecting a child. I only knew for certain this morning. I thought you should know right away.'

Mother covered her mouth with her hands, but her grin poked out on both sides. She shook her head, nodded, and then she wrapped Clara in a hug.

'Our Andrew will have to come home now, won't he? Oh, Clara, you have made me so very happy. Perhaps you have heard that I do not do well with loss? Bless you for giving me something wonderful to occupy my mind. And until Andrew comes home it will be our secret.'

They chatted about the baby while Clara finished her breakfast. Then she left Mother with dreams of holding her grandchild and went to Andrew's office.

She tapped on the door, but did not wait for permission to enter. She found Miles sitting in Andrew's chair with his feet propped on the desk.

The temptation to slap them off was nearly too much to resist. It grated on her that he was not in his own office. He had one here, as he did in London.

'What is it you wish to speak with me about?'

He sat up taller, and put his feet on the floor where they belonged.

'Clara, I understand that we all deal with grief in our own ways, but I must insist that you stop acting as if Andrew will come through the front door at any moment. He is dead. The sooner we all accept it, the sooner we can move on.'

'Move on? Dismiss your brother as if…?' She had to curl her hands into fists. For her baby's sake she forced herself to relax. She would not give in to the rage making her fingers itch.

'You are a widow, good sister. You must accept it at some point.'

'Until I weep over my husband's body I will continue to believe he is making his way home. You, good brother, may not tell me otherwise.'

'I never realised how stubborn you are.'

'It is something I was forced to learn.'

He glanced away for a moment. It was evident he recognised his own part in her learning that trait. Now he would have to deal with it.

'You are my brother's widow. I am responsible for your care.'

'If the day comes when I am a widow, you will *not* be responsible for me or for my children.'

'Like it or not, you will need me.'

That statement shook her. She had managed on her own before, but barely. How would she do it with an infant at her breast?

She was not foolish enough to believe that Miles had her family's wellbeing in mind. He had ruined them once before and he would do it again. Why wouldn't he? She knew the truth of his crimes. It would be in his best interests to get rid of her.

And he would do it in a manner which did not make him look a villain in front of his mother.

But as tricky a lout as Miles was, she was the one who had been once bitten. They would see who was the canniest.

One thing he would need to do was keep her out of this office, to prevent her from snooping and discovering what he was up to. To test the theory, she touched the office keys in her pocket, let them jingle.

'I will take your office keys. I believe Andrew gave you a set?' He held out his hand.

She put her hands behind her back. 'I will keep them.'

'I will not indulge you as my brother did. Give me the keys.'

'Why should I trust you to keep Andrew's finances in order? You have given me no reason to do so.'

'I hardly care if you trust me or not. Now that my brother is dead, the finances you speak of are mine.'

Impatience was not a normal expression for Miles. She had never known him to do anything but hide his negative emotions behind a magnetic smile.

'The keys, Clara.'

'Very well.' She reached into her pocket, pulled them out, and then set them on the desk with a slap. 'I suppose I will have to put the past behind me and trust you.'

He smiled, his emotions once again veiled. 'Indeed. You need not worry.'

Indeed? Without a doubt he meant her family harm.

Andrew might yet come home and save them all. She was not ready to admit he would not. But if he did not... No, not that. In the meantime, until he did come home, it was up to her to protect her husband's fortune.

'If you need anything, Miles—any help in finding where Andrew keeps things—you may call on me. I will be in the parlour, embroidering roses.'

'A worthy occupation for a lady, Clara.'

With a shrug, she went out of the office, closing the door behind her.

Two steps to the left of the door was a painting. She reached behind it and withdrew the spare set of office keys that Andrew kept there. She slipped them into the bodice of her gown.

Do not worry, Andrew. She directed the thought to… Well, she did not know where. Except that it was not Heavenward, since that was not where Andrew was. *That low-down brother of yours will not get the best of us. Not this time.*

It was after midnight when Clara crept downstairs, the keys wrapped in a handkerchief stuffed into her pocket to ensure they were well hidden and did not jingle.

Passing by Miles's chamber, she stopped to listen. The man snored loud enough to cover any noise her steps might make. Good, then. It ought to be safe enough to be in the office for a few hours.

Sitting at the desk, she opened a drawer, withdrew a writing tablet. Having sat beside Andrew and Joseph Billings, watching all they did, she was confident she could keep track of the expenses going out and the funds coming in.

In the morning she would send what she had found to Billings. He could keep track of things at his home in the village. Neither she nor the accountant would recognise Miles's authority to withdraw his employment. And when Andrew returned he would have an orderly accounting of the estate and the business.

What she needed to do was discover what crooked thing Miles was doing—because surely he was. A false set of books, she imagined. Perhaps he meant to hide what the estate was worth to decrease what she would receive if it was determined Andrew was… gone.

Her mind recoiled at the thought.

It simply could not be.

So far disaster had not been determined. No person of authority had paid them a grim visit.

She pulled on drawer handles looking for those which were locked. Oddly, none were. Perhaps he was too wily for that. A locked drawer would indicate a secret. Even believing he was the only one with access to the office, he would be cautious.

She pushed away from the desk and stood up, walked in a slow circle about the room. Surely something would present itself…something would look odd or out of order.

Something such as that book which was out of alphabetical order. 'W' did not belong before 'A' in any well-kept bookcase.

She took it down, opened the cover. Loose pages nearly fell out, but she caught them.

What on earth?

Scanning them, she realised it had not taken Miles long to indulge in old habits.

Clara carried the book to the desk. She smoothed open a ledger page which was a copy of Mrs Benton's allowance, along with another which reflected Clara's funds—the small bit of money she'd had when she'd come into her marriage.

Of all the low-down, miserable things to do… Miles had made notations that made it appear as if Clara was taking his mother's money and putting it into her own account.

At this rate she would appear to be a wealthy woman in no time at all. On paper, only. Money was not changing from one place to another—it only appeared as if it was.

Very clearly, Miles meant to accuse her of theft. If Andrew returned, he would show him how, in his absence, she had taken advantage of his mother. If he did not return, it would be used as an excuse to have her turned away from the estate.

Carefully, in the exact order she had found them, she placed the fake pages back in the book.

There was not much she could do about Miles's dishonesty for now. But what she would do was make honest entries and have them sent over to Joseph Billings each morning.

She set the book back in its incorrect spot.

Going out of the office, she locked the door behind her.

'You will not beat me this time,' she whispered when she passed Miles's chamber.

No matter what else happened, she would not be swindled again.

Chapter Eleven

Not even a mile from home, and yet it felt like a hundred. Andrew plucked his foot from a puddle of the thick, gooey mud which clung to his boot as if it intended to keep him from going that final distance.

But why should mud be any different from any other obstacle which had thrown itself in his way?

A wicked weather system had begun it all. Had it not been for the storm, he would have been home a day ahead of schedule. Severe winds had blown his ship far off course, and eventually landed them in a remote place.

Still and all, it might have been much worse. The ship had nearly gone down at one point. The waves had been violent. His ship had nearly collided with another. It had been a harrowing event which had left the crew shaken. They'd all shouted a great huzzah when the ship had run aground. There had been damage to the hull, but they were all alive and grateful.

The first thing he had wanted to do was send a message home, advising Clara that he was delayed. But he'd had no idea where the nearest town might be. Even if he had, the weather had been too severe for him to go exploring. Even if there had been telegraph lines, the wires would have been blown down. The post was not likely to be operating either.

After three days the weather had cleared enough for him to send someone to find a village. As he'd thought, there had been no way of communication.

He would have simply taken off for home on foot had he not had an injured crewman to see to. Had he not needed to arrange for repairs to the ship.

Andrew had found himself stuck. He'd tried to hire a lad to carry a message home, but to no avail. Everyone had been occupied dealing with the damage the storm had done.

Eventually he'd been able to leave the place he had been stranded in, but it had been slow going because the blasted rain and wind had begun again.

This morning a friendly farmer had come upon him and given him a ride to a village. There, the farmer insisted his animals had been hard pressed all day and could go no further.

No matter—home was not so far away. And at least the rain had let up, so the walk home was not as miserable as it might have been if he did not mind mud.

With every sucking step, he minded it more.

At last he saw the windows of home, glowing yellow and welcoming. So close and yet it seemed still so very far away. And he was all but crawling to get to it.

It was not impossible that he would expire of exposure before he reached the front door.

Step, pluck, step...

It went on and on. Only one thing kept him moving forward.

Clara. What must she be thinking? She would know that his ship had not make port in London.

More than a week had passed since he should have been home. No doubt his wife was desperate with worry. Several times along the way he'd tried to send a wire, but always it had been the same thing...telegraph wires blown down...the post unavailable.

What time was it, anyway? It had been dusk when the farmer had dropped him off in the village.

It was time to be home—that was what it was.

Once again it had rained all day. Now it was dark, and the clouds had blown away, allowing moonlight to shine upon the soggy land.

Clara went to her window, the same way she did every night to watch the road. Done for the day, she stooped to take off her shoes and stockings.

Her maid would be along soon, but until she came, Clara would occupy her position beside the window.

Miles wished for her to accept what he believed to be the truth—that her husband was not returning. He had called her stubborn because she would not.

It was true. She was stubborn. However, tenacious was a better word. Yes, tenacious was more hopeful.

Until she had proof, or a visit from someone who might have it, she would stay right where she was and watch out of this window, which had an excellent view of the road.

She touched her stomach. At least she was not watching alone. If it came to the worst—it would not, but just in case—she would have a part of her husband.

However, she was not nearly ready to give up on believing that this might be the night she slept in his arms once again.

But wait! What was that?

A movement on the road had caught her eye. It was so far off that it appeared no more than a blur. Probably Thor on his nightly walk.

She strained her eyes, because the closer the figure came, the more she thought it had two legs, not four.

Pressing her nose to the glass, she decided it was human. A male human. Who was having trouble walking in the mud.

Why would anyone be walking in the mud at night unless...?

And why would his stride look so like...?

'Andrew!' she gasped.

She ran out of the chamber, down the corridor. Her maid was coming towards her.

'Della! Please tell Mrs Benton that Andrew is on the drive!'

'All the saints be praised!'

Della hurried down the hallway towards Mrs Benton's room.

Clara did not even feel her feet on the stairs. Perhaps she was flying.

She dashed out through the front door, waving her arm madly.

'Andrew!' she shouted.

Even though it was too dark to see his features, she knew this was her husband. She was not dreaming him this time.

'Clara!'

Lifting her skirt, she dashed down the steps. Cold, squishy mud welled between her toes.

Oh, but no matter! It only served to prove this moment was real and Andrew was actually running towards her.

'Andrew!' she cried again as he picked her up and swung her about.

She hung on tight to his neck, squeezed hard, not quite believing this could be true...that his arms around her were solid and not a dream...that her toes really were dangling in the air and not treading a dream.

'I'm sorry, Clara,' he said between kisses. 'I will never go away again.'

'Do not even try. Oh, sweet mercy, Andrew... There was a rumour that your ship had sunk. That all aboard were lost.'

He did not set her down, but shifted her weight and carried her towards the front door.

'We went aground. One of the crew was injured but is recovering.'

'I told everyone you were coming home.'

'And here I am. I've never been so cold in my life.'

'Don't worry. It will be my single objective to warm you up.'

Coming into the hall the first person they saw was his mother in her night clothes, hurrying down the stairs.

Andrew set Clara down.

A maid hurried into the parlour with an armload of towels.

Word of Andrew's arrival was spreading quickly. Good news had a way of doing that.

'Oh, Andrew!' Mother exclaimed, her arms open

wide. He hurried forward, stepped into her embrace. 'Oh, my son. Clara would not allow me to believe you were dead.'

'I was only delayed. And it feels like heaven now, being home with all of you.'

'Come to the parlour, my dearest. The fire is already being revived.'

'I should change. I'm bringing mud to the floor.'

'I cannot let you out of my sight. A little mud won't hurt anything.'

Her mother-in-law was right. Mud did not matter. Only one thing did.

The man they all loved was home. When it had seemed it would never happen, here he was.

A grinning servant rushed from the parlour.

'Oh, welcome home, sir!' he declared, hurrying on his way.

'I will run to the kitchen and find you something warm to drink…broth,' Clara said.

Before she did, she turned to hug him one more time. Yes, he was still flesh-and-blood reality.

'Oh, Andrew!' Her voice came out on a sob of pure, absolute joy. 'Go and sit by the fire and get warm.'

'Someone get Miles and tell him to come to the parlour at once.' Andrew's mother sat down in the chair beside her son, snatched up his hand and held it to her heart.

Clara dashed towards the kitchen.

The household, which had been settling for the night, was coming alive with excitement.

Andrew's office door opened. Miles stepped into the corridor. 'Is it true?' he asked. 'A parlour maid has said so, but has my brother returned?'

'Quite true.' Peering past his shoulder, Clara spotted a stack of papers on the desk. A book lay open on top of them...*the* book.

Apparently he was not going to waste a moment before he exposed her 'crime' against Mrs Benton.

'But I heard the boat perished. I did not make that up. Clearly I heard wrong... But is he well?'

'He is cold, but not injured, and not ill as far as I can tell.'

Miles exhaled, nodded. A small smile played at the corners of his mouth. His expression was as unguarded as she had ever seen it. He truly was glad his brother had come home safe and hale.

'Andrew is in the parlour with your mother. I am going to the kitchen to get him some broth.'

Dashing away for the broth, she did not feel relieved. It was not a surprise that Miles loved his brother. She knew that already. His love for Andrew did not mean he no longer wished to be rid of her. She knew his secrets. Although Andrew also knew them, Miles could hardly get rid of his own brother.

Well, he was not getting rid of her either.

As luck would have it, Lilly and her young beau were coming into the kitchen, looking flushed from being outside…and in love.

'Peter, thank goodness you are here.'

He glanced at Lilly, a red blush flushing all the way to his ears.

'Is it true?' Lilly asked. 'Andrew has come home?'

Clara hugged her sister, because in spite of Miles, she had never been so happy. She knew Lilly would be, too.

'It is true.' She let go of her sister, then turned to young Peter. 'I need your help and in a hurry. Will you go to the village and bring the accountant here? Tell him Andrew has returned. He will know the situation is urgent.'

'Yes, of course, Mrs Benton. I will go straight away.'

Given the conditions on the road, it might take him some time. But hopefully Billings would get here before Miles presented his lies.

Andrew had not even half finished his broth before Miles insisted they go to his office and discuss something he seemed to think was more urgent than sitting here in peace and soaking up the warmth from the fire.

'I am certain it can wait until morning. Now I just want to be with my family.'

'Shall I wake the children?' Clara asked, standing behind his chair with her hands on his shoulders.

Perhaps she thought he would drift away if she did not anchor him. After all this time and effort to get home, it did still seem dreamlike.

'No, my love, let them sleep.'

'There is a matter of some urgency,' Miles said. 'I believe it is best dealt with tonight.'

Miles did not look at him when he said so, but at Clara.

'Very well.' Andrew squeezed his wife's hands, then stood, went to where his mother sat and kissed her cheek. 'I won't be long.'

'Take as long as you wish, my boy. I am coming with you.'

'You will be bored silly, Mother. Stay here with Clara.' Miles smiled as he spoke, but it seemed to Andrew that the gesture was strained.

'Oh, no, I am not staying here either. I, and your mother, have been separated from Andrew too long as it is. I am certain whatever you have to say will be fascinating. If Mother and I grow bored, we will check to see that all the books are in alphabetical order.'

Miles opened his mouth as if he had something else

to say, but then closed it, his lips pressed into a thin, tight line—which was unusual for him.

Mother frowned. 'That sounds as dull as ditch water, my girl. I know of something much nicer we can discuss.'

An odd glance passed between the women he loved. Some sort of secret, unless he missed his guess. A secret which made their eyes twinkle.

There was no time to discover what it was at the moment because Miles, having been so eager to retire to the office, now stood next to the desk without speaking.

Andrew stood in front of the fireplace, because in spite of the broth he was only half warmed. It would take Clara's promise to get the job done.

'Miles? Here we are in my office. Please tell us what business you wish to discuss.'

For a matter so urgent, his brother now seemed reluctant to reveal what it was. 'This is best discussed without the ladies present,' Miles insisted.

'But I adore business matters, Miles,' Clara said. 'I shall remain here.'

'And I shall as well,' his mother said. 'Hurry on with it, Miles. Not everything is about dreary business.'

Again, that odd, twinkling glance passed between his wife and his mother.

His brother's expression did not twinkle. His face alternated between bleached white and…was it green?

'Are you ill, Miles?' he asked. 'Shall we continue in the morning?'

'It would be a shame not to know what is so urgent. We would not wish to lose sleep over it,' Clara said. 'Miles? We are eager to hear what you have to say.'

Mother went to Miles and patted his cheek. 'My dear sweet boy… I say we simply get it out of the way so we can discuss more important things. Don't you agree, Daughter?'

'We must leave it up to Miles.' Clara picked up a stack of papers from the desk. She handed them to his brother with a snap. 'Only he knows what is so urgent.'

Miles gripped the papers in his fist. He tapped them on his open palm, all the while gazing at their mother. It was the oddest expression, Andrew thought. Love, regret, all mixed with a sheen of moisture in his eyes.

'But you are ill, my dearest,' said his mother. 'It shows all over your face. Shall I call for the doctor? I wonder if all the excitement has undone you?'

'No, Mother. I am well enough. Forgive me for making you fear I was not.'

Miles walked to the hearth, stared at the flames for a moment, and then, with a slight nod at Clara, tossed the papers in. Fingers of flame caught them, curled the ends and then burned the papers to ash.

'Was that what was so urgent, Brother?'

'I meant to discuss something with you. I wanted to do it before I spoke to our mother about it.'

'It will save time if you tell us both at the same time,' his mother pointed out.

'It is only...only that I wish to make a trip to Belgium. Soon. That is what I wished to discuss with you.'

'Belgium? Oh, my dear, you have only been home a short time.' Mother gave Miles a hug. 'But young men have a need for adventure, I suppose.'

In Belgium? thought Andrew. France seemed more likely.

Before he could ask about it, someone else rushed into the office.

'Billings? 'What brings you here so late?'

Miles looked as if he was sweating. Surely his brother *was* ill, despite his denials?

The accountant glanced at Clara, who gave a subtle shrug. If he had not known her so well, he would not have seen it.

'I heard from a farmer in the village that you had returned. I wanted to see for myself.'

'It was kind of you to come,' Clara said. 'It must be a relief for you to see that all is well. You must stay until morning. We shall have a chamber prepared for you.'

'Indeed, do stay, Billings. We shall catch up on the accounts first thing in the morning,' Andrew said.

'It will be good to get back to them.'

'Have you been absent?'

Billings frowned at Miles.

This evening was so full of odd glances that Andrew could not keep up. The only glance he knew he was getting right was the simmering one his wife kept flashing him.

'I was ill for a time, but I am now recovered,' said Billings. 'Your wife has done an excellent job of making copies of all receipts and sending them to me. Everything will be in order.'

'Please excuse me. I must retire to my chamber,' Miles said.

'Wait, Miles,' Clara said, going to his brother. She squeezed his arm and smiled at him. 'Please stay for a few minutes more.'

Miles's eyes went wide in apparent surprise.

No doubt his own expression was as surprised as his brother's.

More had happened while he was away than anyone was saying. But he would get to the bottom of whatever it was later, after his wife had warmed him up.

Clara and his mother withdrew to a corner, whispered for a moment. Then they returned to the hearth, arms linked.

'Andrew, your mother has something to tell you.'

'It is the most marvellous news. Clara has allowed me to be the one to reveal it… Andrew, you are to be a father.'

Clara was beside him before the thought could sink in.

'You are expecting?' he asked stupidly. Because of course she would be. 'We are having…a baby?'

He wrapped her up in his arms, held her tight and wept. It might not be the manliest behaviour, but he had been gone so long that many people must have given up on him, presumed him to be lost.

Not Clara, though. And because of her faith Mother had not given up either.

As soon as he'd let go of her Miles was there to wrap him in a hug. Patting Andrew on the back, he said, 'Congratulations, Brother.'

Joseph Billings stepped forward to shake his hand. 'Well done, Mr Benton.'

And Lilly must have been listening at the door, because he heard her screech half a second before she burst into the office.

After dozens of hugs all about, their happy tears gave way to laughter.

A chambermaid entered and whispered to Clara.

'A bath is prepared in your chamber, Andrew,' she relayed.

He no longer felt cold, but a hot bath would be just the thing.

And then there was nothing he wanted more than to be alone with his wife, to celebrate their good news privately.

'Clara?'

Miles's voice came from behind them as she and Andrew began the climb to their chamber, arms locked and heads bent for a kiss.

'I am sorry to interrupt, but may I have a word?'

'Now?' Andrew asked.

It was hard to miss the frustration in his voice. Ever since their reunion they'd wanted nothing more than to be alone. It seemed like one delay after another.

'It is important or I would not ask. Clara will explain it to you, Andrew, if she wishes. But please, good sister, just a moment is all I ask.'

'Go and begin your bath.' She went up on her toes to whisper, 'I will join you before the water cools.'

Without a word between them, she and Miles watched Andrew climb the stairs. When he reached the top of the stairway and turned right down the corridor, Miles made a sound from deep in his chest. It seemed like something between a sigh and a grunt.

'You really do love my brother,' he said.

She slid him a sidelong glance, nodded. 'I imagine it shows.'

'It shows in him too. Funny…he was the last person I thought would fall in love.' He shrugged, gave her half a smile. Then he shook his head. 'But that isn't what I…'

Miles looked uncommonly nervous—as if he would rather flee than stand here with her. 'You knew what I intended to do?'

She did, and there was no point in denying it. 'Andrew kept a spare set of keys so…yes, of course I was aware.'

'Of course. I should have guessed you would not let me cheat you again. You will think I am the worst person alive…and perhaps I am. You are well within your rights to hate me.'

'Except that you did not act on what you meant to do.'

'I could not, in the end.'

'I suppose, coming face to face with the consequences, you thought better of hurting your mother. Anyone can see how much you love her.'

'Perhaps not as much as you do. Or maybe it is that you have a better sort of love.'

Miles glanced up at the empty staircase, probably not wanting her to notice the moisture standing in his eyes.

'At any time you could have exposed me to my mother for what I did to you after Spencer died, and yet you did not. I lost sleep every night, thinking that you would.'

'If you wish to know the truth, I did want to. But you and I share a common bond when it comes to your mother. We both love her and would never say anything to harm her.'

'Tonight I nearly did… I meant to be rid of you even if it cost my mother's heart. I had never fully taken into account the result of what I was about to do.' He stared at the floor, then jerked his gaze back at her. 'But then, when I realised that you knew what I intended to do and yet you did not reveal me… No, you even dared me to go through with it, didn't you? Well, you demonstrated what love is. Made me aware that I do not feel it.'

'Clearly you do have it, or you would have followed through. Miles, I did believe that in the end you would do the honourable thing.'

'Truly? There is no reason you should have.'

'I knew you loved your mother. Besides, even if you'd made the wrong choice, I would have been able to prove my innocence. But I was praying all along that you would do the right thing and I would not have to. Do you know, when you tossed those papers in the fire I nearly cheered for you?'

'Why? I do not understand. It would have been your chance to be rid of me. Andrew would never allow me to stay if he knew what I'd planned to do.'

'Planning and doing are not the same thing.'

'But I did you wrong—grievous wrong that first time. Back then it was out of greed, I confess. This time it was out of fear. I was certain that at some point you were going to expose me. With Andrew gone, I saw my chance to make certain you did not.'

Miles sat down heavily on the bottom stair. His shoulders slumped.

'The worst of it is, I liked you, and I ruined you anyway. I have no right to ask your forgiveness, so I will not. But just know that I regret what I did…and what I nearly did.'

Clara sat beside him. 'What you did to me and my children was horrible… I will never deny it. But can I forgive you? Yes, I believe I can.'

'I cannot imagine why.'

'For one thing, you say you regret your crime against me. I believe you, Miles, and so I forgive you.'

The moisture in his eyes leaked out in a single tear that rolled down his cheek. She did not think she'd made a mistake in believing him to be repentant.

'I would not be as kind to someone who had wronged me,' he said.

'You might, if the wrong done to you had led you

to the place you wanted to be. Truly, I am happy with my life as it is. If the past had been different, I would never have ended up marrying your brother. Had I not faced the challenges I did, I would not have been the person Andrew would fall in love with. All that made me stronger. And I think I like myself better now than I did then.'

'I'm glad for you, then. I cannot say the same of myself. I am my father's child, and as much as my mother adored him, he was a flawed soul. But I promise you something: I have learned from all this. I will strive to be a better man.'

'I believe that too.'

He gave her a watery blink. 'Because I said so? Aren't you worried that I am charming you into forgiving me?'

She laughed. 'You are not all that charming, Miles. And I am quite immune to it. But are you really going away?'

'It would be for the best. Once you tell Andrew about all this he will not want me around.'

'You might be surprised to know how much he cares for you.' She stood up. 'I must go up now. But I hope if you do decide to leave you will come back in time to welcome your niece or nephew.'

'Clara…' Miles's voice caught her halfway up the stairs. 'My brother is a lucky man.'

'Indeed he is.'

And he was about to get luckier...

By the time Clara entered their chamber Andrew was asleep in the bath, his head back and his long arms draped over the sides.

A wet washcloth lay on his chest. Apparently he had begun to wash and then fallen asleep.

Clara pulled a stool to the edge of the tub. She sat down, carefully lifted the cloth. She dipped it in the water, which was still slightly warm.

She had been delayed coming up, but the time she'd spent speaking with Miles had been important—not only to bring peace between the two of them but to the rest of the family.

Only half of Andrew's hair was wet. He must have fallen asleep before he'd finished washing it.

The poor man had gone through an ordeal, getting home to them. Indeed, they had all gone through an ordeal waiting for him, as well. It was impossible that they would never be separated again over the years, but this was now, and here he was, and here she was.

Life was good. It was blessed beyond what she had ever dreamed.

Gently, she trickled water through the strands of his hair, not sure whether to be patient and let him sleep or to wake him and make up for some of the time they had lost.

Dribbling water over his face, she whispered, 'I love you more than you can guess.'

'Ah... I think I can guess.'

His eyes blinked open. The warm brown shimmer in them made her blood feel as if hot syrup was sliding from her heart to her fingers...and to her mouth.

'It cannot have been an easy thing to love me enough not to give me up as dead,' he said.

She bent over the tub and kissed his wet lips. 'I will confess it was hard at times, and at other times it was nearly impossible. But there was your mother to think of, so I pushed though.'

And there was the baby. She'd refused to accept that it was an orphan before it was even born.

'I tried to get word to you, but the telegraph lines were down all the way from there to here. And the post was a mess. I came as fast as I could.'

'And here you are, safely home at last.' She trailed her fingers along the cords of his throat, over the line of his shoulder.

He sat up. Water sloshed over the edges of the tub when he leaned over the side to cup her face and kiss her.

'My gown is getting wet.'

'Take it off.'

A gust of wind shook the window in its frame.

'You got home just in time,' she said, as she removed her gown and everything else.

'Not soon enough.'

He slid to one end of the tub as best he could, to make room for her. More water sloshed over the side when she got in. It was a tight fit—nearly more limbs than water now.

'Something was going on earlier,' he said. 'So many looks going back and forth I was getting dizzy. It had to do with Miles, I presume?'

'Except for the looks to your mother about the baby, yes, it had to do with him.'

'I fear to ask what…' He ran his fingers over her cheek, letting water drops slip down her cheek and then her throat. 'But let's get it out of the way. I want to spend time talking about our child.'

'Miles faced temptation and overcame it. He believes you will be angry and put him out of the house, but I told him you loved him.'

'What temptation?'

'I difficult one. He feared that one day I would tell your mother what he had done before…when I was a widow. With you gone, he thought he could get rid of me—and the risk. What he meant to do was make it look as if I was stealing from your mother. When it came down to it, he found he could not carry through.'

She felt Andrew's muscles tense. He lunged up suddenly, looming over her with his fists clenched. She smiled because, angry or not, he was a sight she would never forget. Was that really steam lifting from his bare, dripping limbs, even though the water was not hot enough for steam?

'I shall kill him.'

She splashed at his knees, laughed. 'No, you won't. Miles and I have made our peace. You will be the man your father taught you to be and do the same.'

'Yes, I suppose so—after I kill him.'

Slowly he sat down. Still, he seemed rather steamy… in a way which was morphing from anger into something more appropriate for the situation.

'You have made peace with him? Truly?'

'Yes, truly. Now, enough talk of murder.'

She wriggled her toes on his belly, because her toes were the only part of her free to move. Other than her fingers. She would take a moment to decide how to use those…

'How did you do that?' he asked.

Yes, his eyes were heating rather nicely. His gaze made the water feel warmer than it was.

'You know how,' she told him. 'Love is stronger than hate. I love you all so dearly. So does Miles. And there you have it.'

'You make it sound so simple.'

'Well, it is…and it isn't.' She leaned forward and kissed him. 'Let's talk about our baby.'

'With great pleasure, dear wife. Are you feeling well?'

'Sometimes wonderful and sometimes awful. But always grateful.'

'Me, too. So grateful I cannot believe I am the same man who knocked on your door that first time.'

'I remember him. The one who insisted upon marrying me and doing so without falling in love.'

'The one who thought he knew it all and actually knew nothing until this beautiful…' he touched her lips, her neck, then kissed her in the places he touched '…exquisitely lovely and intelligent woman came along and taught him he was wrong.'

'You are the one who came along.' She gripped the sides of the tub, wriggled about so she could stand. 'I only had the good sense to go with you.'

Andrew grinned up at her, while this time she dripped upon him.

'You are shivering,' he said. 'Are you cold?'

'Not a bit. But I believe you will be if you do not follow me to bed.'

Stepping out of the tub, she picked up the towel and dried herself with it.

Finished, she handed the towel down to him. He stood, but instead of taking the towel he indicated with a glance at his wet limbs that she should dry him, as well.

'You do such a fine job of it,' he said, arching a brow, lifting one muscular arm.

'It's a fine bold man you are, Andrew Benton, expecting to be pampered…indulged…'

He nodded, grinned, and then turned his back to be dried there too.

'And coddled…' He turned about. 'Fondled, perhaps?'

She tossed the towel on top of his head, laughed and dashed away.

Oh, but he was quick. He caught her arm and drew her to him. Then he picked her up, threw her on the bed, then dived on top of her.

'Oh, my… It is a fine bold man you are, indeed.'

Christmas Eve, one year and a few months later

Clara held her baby daughter in her arms. She was pointing to a candle on the Christmas tree which was so tall it nearly brushed the parlour ceiling.

Annabeth caught the chubby, grasping hand. 'Hot! Clarissa, we do not touch the flame,' she said, giving her sister the same admonition she had just been given.

'May she play with my new puppy?' George asked.

'No, my boy. That would be unkind to the dog. Has

your tutor left for the holiday? Ask him to remain for dinner if he is still here.'

Clara and Andrew had decided against sending George away to school. Perhaps in a few years they would send him, but for now it was wide open spaces and the company of animals that suited him best.

George dashed away with the pup under his arm, its tail waving like a mad little flag.

In Clara's opinion this moment, here in the parlour, was a slice of paradise. Even though outside the wind raged, and the rain blew in sheets against the windows, inside the fire danced cheerfully.

'Look over there, Clarissa.' Clara pointed her finger, so the baby would know where to look. 'See Papa and Grandmama playing the piano. Doesn't it sound pretty?'

The piano had arrived last week. Andrew and his mother were both learning to play, and it was among the happiest of sounds she ever heard.

His mother paused. 'If only Miles was here,' she said. 'He has a fine voice and he could sing along with us.'

Miles had actually gone to Belgium. His letters were few and brief, but in them he claimed to be doing well. Hopefully it was true. They would not know for certain until he returned home one day and they saw for themselves.

Andrew had asked his brother to come for Christmas—he had a new niece to meet, after all. And of course his mother missed him.

Miles had not answered his brother's letter, so perhaps he was coming and perhaps he was not.

Perhaps he was fine and perhaps he was not.

What a great gift it would be for his mother if he did come, though.

Her mother-in-law turned on the piano bench. She tugged on Andrew's sleeve. 'It is time, don't you think?' she said.

'A few more moments,' he answered. 'I believe I hear the carriage on the drive. Lilly must be home from London. I would like her to be here for this moment.'

"I believe she came in half an hour ago."

But be here for what moment? It sounded mysterious… But Christmas and secrets went together in the nicest way.

Andrew's mother stood up from the piano, walked across the room and held out her arms for the baby. Clara handed her over to be cuddled against her grandmother's bosom, then she crossed the room and sat beside Andrew on the piano bench.

'I know your secret, Andrew.'

'What secret?'

The one he was grinning over, she thought.

'The one Mother just hinted at.'

'I doubt it—but what do you think?'

He placed his arm about her shoulder, drew her in and kissed the tip of her nose.

'You missed.' She lifted her lips to make his target obvious.

'Ah, yes…how errant of me.'

With one large, wonderful finger under her chin, he lifted it and gave her a proper kiss, a promise of things to come.

'You are going to hire a piano instructor? Is that it?'

'I ought to—but that is not it.'

Voices, sounding excited, came from the direction of the hall.

Lilly and her young stable hand came in, flushed with cold and excitement.

'I…we have an announcement to make,' Lilly said.

'Well?' Mrs Benton said. 'We are on pins to know the happy news.'

'Peter is going to ask Andrew for my hand.'

'Indeed? Well, then, young man. Come into my office where we can discuss this properly.'

Lilly was all but dancing on her toes, watching the men leave the room.

'Sit here with me, Sister.' Clara patted the piano bench. 'Are you certain about this? Peter is as fine a young man as they come, but you always wanted a noble society husband.'

'That was an immature attitude. Now I am in love

and I see matters more clearly. You were right, Clara. Love matters more than some silly social position. I will be deliriously happy to be Mrs Peter Goods.'

'Did you hear that, Clarissa?' Mrs Benton tickled her granddaughter under her fat little chin and earned a giggle for her efforts. 'Pay attention to the way your aunt is choosing the very best thing.'

The men were back within a quarter-hour.

'He approves,' Peter announced.

'Heartily,' Andrew said, and set a stack of papers on the hearth mantel.

Clara sent for champagne. A toast was in order. This was a day of days.

They had their glasses lifted, tilted, and ready to toast when two more people entered the parlour.

'You are expecting me?' Miles asked, coming inside with a young lady clutching his elbow.

'Miles!' His mother crossed the room and placed the baby in Clara's arms.

Turning to her long-absent son, she gave him a long, tearful hug, all the while giving the clinging stranger a curious glance along with a welcoming smile.

'Hello, my dear, and welcome to our home,' she said. And then his mother did what came so naturally to her and gave the stranger a hug.

It never ceased to amaze Clara how Mrs Benton could love someone at first sight. How she never saw anything but good in everyone.

'Welcome home, Brother. And you have brought a guest?' Andrew said, extending a hand in greeting to the lady, who smiled as warmly as if she were not a stranger at all.

'Not a guest so much, really...'

Miles had the oddest look on his face. Not an expression Clara had ever seen before. This was not the same man who had gone to Belgium last year. But who was he now...and why was he so changed?

'May I introduce Mary? Mary Holmes...my wife.'

Clara was the first to recover from the stunning surprise. While the rest of the family blinked, mouths hanging agape, Clara waived to the maid for more flutes and champagne.

'Welcome to the family, Mary,' Andrew said. 'Forgive us for being momentarily surprised. We had no idea...'

'Who would?' his mother exclaimed. 'But I promise, Mary, we are simply thrilled!'

Mother finished her drink in a gulp, then used her free hand to hug her new daughter-in-law—this time as a beloved family member.

'Even if we did miss the wedding,' Mother went on. 'We shall have a grand celebration of our own.'

Clara was reminded of the first time she and her family had been welcomed by Mrs Benton. Complete and unconditional love from the very first.

'And we thought *our* announcement would be the

surprise of the evening,' Lilly said with a laugh. 'Or the year. We have just announced our engagement, Mary.'

'How perfectly wonderful!' Their new relative clapped her hands. 'I must apologise for stealing your moment.'

Clara decided she liked Mary quite well. She was not a bit shy and seemed to be a happy soul.

'The more Christmas surprises the better,' Clara declared.

'I lift my glass to that,' Andrew added.

'I have been thinking for hours upon hours how we would explain it all, but now… Well, the truth of it is I was desperate to meet you all.' Mary shrugged, pressing closer Miles. 'And when one travels with a minister, it is only proper to be wed to him.'

Even Clara was too stunned to speak this time.

'And so there you have it…us,' Miles said. 'I am not ordained yet, though, so I am not a proper man of the cloth.'

Proper man of the cloth? Surely Clara had not heard correctly.

'Miles is being trained under my father, who is ordained,' said Mary. 'But we wished to marry anyway, and so we did. Father would not have let me come otherwise. And I so very badly wanted to meet every one of you.'

'And we would have wished to meet you too, Mary,'

Clara said, her voice finally recovered, 'had we known of you.'

'I told Miles he must write and tell you everything, but he said that in light of his past sins you would never believe it.'

No one quite knew how to respond to that, because it was very likely they would not.

Miles? A minister? Or soon to be one?

'Shall we sit?' Clara suggested.

If any more surprises came along she did not wish to drop the baby.

Andrew and Miles went to stand in front of the hearth, spoke quietly to one another. Clara could only imagine what sort of conversation it was.

All any of them had ever hoped for was that Miles would not resume a life of crime while in Belgium.

'Would it be all right if I held my niece?' Mary asked.

Clara handed the baby over, still feeling that this was some sort of Christmas dream from which she was about to pop awake.

'I wonder what is the most shocking to you,' Mary said, while smiling at Clarissa. 'The fact that Miles is a married man or that he is a minister in training.'

'It would be the part about him being a minister.'

'You may take the credit for that, Clara. Miles rented a room from my family when he first came to Belgium. He and my father began to talk. Miles says that when you forgave him for swindling you it made him see life in a new way. One thing led to another, spiritually speaking, and he found his calling.'

'I admit that I am stunned—but in the nicest way. I hope you will be very happy together.'

'We will be! Poor as church mice, though. At least for a time. My husband wishes to repay that other widow what he robbed her of.'

My word...

Clara found she liked Mary more and more. She was not blinded by her husband's character...or former character, as it seemed...and she loved him anyway. If Miles ever tried to get away with anything he was bound to fail.

'And given we will live in and minister to the part of London you used to live in, we will struggle. But it is what he needs, I think. It will prove to him that he is not his father's shadow.'

'Welcome to the family, Mary. We could not be more pleased to have you as one of us,' she said, quite truthfully.

'That means so much to me. And it will to Miles. Oh, look...' Mary nodded to the hearth, where Andrew and Miles now embraced. 'Your good husband forgives him.'

'Andrew has always loved his brother. And both of them love their mother.'

'I am certain I shall take to her...perhaps I have already.'

The next half an hour went by with Clara getting better acquainted with her new sister-in-law. She barely noticed Andrew tapping her on the shoulder.

'May I have a word in private, my dear? In my office,' he said holding the papers he had brought clutched between his arm and his ribs.

'If Clarissa gets fretful just hand her to Mrs Benton,' Clara told Mary. 'No one is better at soothing her.'

Clara followed Andrew out of the parlour down the corridor and into his office.

'It is time for your Christmas gift,' he said, grinning broadly.

'Oh, indeed? Shall I lock the door?'

'Perhaps in a moment. But first...' He pressed the official-looking documents into her hand. 'This is for you, Clara. No one deserves it more.'

How curious... How intriguing. Andrew's grin was pleased, but it gave nothing away.

'What is it?'

She shuffled the papers from front to back, back to front—because what was she seeing? Her vision grew blurred as she looked at the impossible words. It was difficult to see through her tears.

'It is the deed to the factory.'

'Frederick Smith has sold you the factory?'

'No, he has sold *you* the factory. Do you see the name on the deed?'

'Clara Benton,' she whispered, wiping at her cheek with her free hand. She was rather certain that no sound was actually ushered from her lips.

'It is yours. You are free to make all the improvements you wish to. I will not meddle in your book-keeping unless you ask me to.'

'Oh, Andrew...' Much too overwhelmed to say a proper thank-you, she simply stared at him, still grinning at her.

Luckily, there was a way of showing her thanks which did not involve her mouth...not saying words, at any rate.

She went to the door, locked it. Then she swept her arm across the shiny wood surface of the desk, clearing it.

Pens clinked to the floor.

Paper whispered down on top of them.

What could be better than her own factory...her own books to keep...and Andrew?

Mostly Andrew...now lifting her onto the desk... whispering that he loved her...demonstrating it with...

Oh, my word...

* * * * *

COMING SOON!

We really hope you enjoyed reading this book. If you're looking for more romance be sure to head to the shops when new books are available on

Thursday 31ˢᵗ August

To see which titles are coming soon, please visit
millsandboon.co.uk/nextmonth

MILLS & BOON

MILLS & BOON®

Coming next month

THE WARRIOR'S RELUCTANT WIFE
Lissa Morgan

'Peredur?'

He froze, turned, and caught his breath. One of the shapes had risen up in the bed and, despite the dimness of the room, he knew it wasn't the maid. Even if the tiring woman would never have addressed him by his name, he recognized Rhianon's voice, her slender form, the cascading fall of her hair.

'I was making sure the fire still burned,' he whispered, startled at the hoarseness of his voice. 'Go back to sleep.'

'What hour is it?'

'What hour?' Peredur shook his head at the strange question. 'I know not. Does it matter?'

There was a little silence. 'No, not really.' Another silence. 'It's just...there are no church bells here to mark the passing of the night.'

Through the dark, the flames picked out the curve of her cheek, the bridge of her nose, her wide brow. Her face seemed paler, her eyes bigger, her lips fuller.

'No, there are no bells,' he responded, his pulse beginning to beat a little faster as the firelight danced at the base of her throat. 'But it must be well past midnight.'

He'd studied her face keenly enough, as they'd sat before that other brazier, on that other midnight, their wedding night. But he hadn't seen her in a shift then, as he did now, nor beheld the smooth, bare skin of her arms. And now, his imagination proceeded to paint a vivid picture of the naked body *below* the shift.

Continue reading
THE WARRIOR'S RELUCTANT WIFE
Lissa Morgan

Available next month
www.millsandboon.co.uk

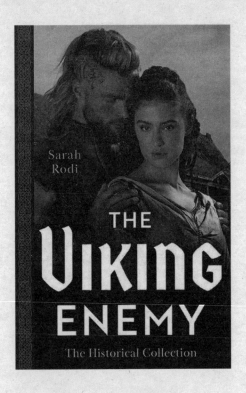